FORTY-DOLLAR BUTTBOY

First Edition

Published by The Nazca Plains Corporation
Las Vegas, Nevada
2009

ISBN: 978-1-935509-48-6

Published by

The Nazca Plains Corporation ®
4640 Paradise Rd, Suite 141
Las Vegas NV 89109-8000

PUBLISHER'S NOTE
Forty-Dollar Buttboy is a work of fiction created wholly by *Jackman Hill's* imagination. All characters are fictional and any resemblance to any persons living or deceased is purely by accident. No portion of this book reflects any real person or events.

Cover Male Photo, Les Byerley
Cover Money Photo, Susan Leggett
Art Director, Blake Stephens

FORTY-DOLLAR BUTTBOY

First Edition

Jackman Hill

CONTENTS

(1)

BUTTBOY

It's kinda a fluke how I ended up in college anyways. I mean, I'm doing okay and all with my classes. One of my professors said I'm naturally smart, just not book smart, and that's enough to get by. But when I say it's a fluke, I mean that I never intended to end up here. No one in my family went to college, and we don't really have a lot of money, so I never even figured it was an option. Then my grandpa kicked the bucket, and it turns out he'd saved up a pension just for me, so I could go to school. He even spelled out what college the money was supposed to go to, and the pension about covered tuition exactly for four years.

So there I was, a white trash punk with a trust fund, suddenly sharing space with all these rich kids. Imagine my surprise. I figured it was a solid chance for me so I tried to take it serious. The first year was hard and I thought I'd flunk out for sure, but I didn't. I even got to be friends with some of the guys around my dorm. They played the same sports as me, and we all went to parties and hung out. It was pretty cool.

My big fuckup came that summer, a few weeks before sophomore year started. I was back in my hometown, working a crap job at a gas station to pay for living expenses, and I was banging this hot girl named Susie who lived in a trailer behind my folks' garage. Well, we weren't always careful, and sure enough, one month into my first semester of my second year as a college boy, she phoned me to say she was pregnant. Shit. And she was gonna keep it. Double shit. I just turned twenty and I had no fuckin' idea what I was gonna do.

I called my Dad, who just yelled at me, so I called my Mom, who gave me this long sigh, and then said, "Travis, you do right by that girl and you send her what money you can." Now I had no feeling that I wanted a kid in my life, and Susie didn't seem keen on me being there either, but I knew she had nothing and I knew that even a little money would help her out. Trouble was, I had none to give. Every cent in my trust fund went to the college, and I'd committed my whole summer earnings to paying for my room and board. I was even living in the same crappy freshman dorm I'd stayed in the year before to save some cash. I had a single—a room to myself—but still, the living situation pretty much sucked.

The idea came up a few nights later, when I was staying up with my buddy Fred, who lives on the same floor as me, down the hall. We finished studying and were in his dorm room smoking weed. Freddie's like me—not a lot of extra dough, which was why he was living the frosh dorm like I was, even though we were both sophomores. We met freshman year and hit it off. I told him my predicament, and he seemed to sympathize. Then, when I asked him how to get some extra cash, he laughed and said: "Well, you can always roll over for them cute little freshman gayboys." I laughed too, but I had no idea what he meant by that remark, and so a few tokes later, I asked him what the fuck he was talking about.

He told me that Cameron, a mutual friend of ours, had made some extra money the previous year by sucking off some of the other guys on our floor, and that he also sometimes got fucked by them. When he first said it I actually couldn't figure out what he was telling me.

"Sucked off? I don't get it. You mean he…"

"He sucked their dicks. Gave 'em head. They even came in his mouth, I think."

I just blinked. "Holy fuck. Really? No shit?"

"Oh yeah," Freddie said, blowing a column of smoke toward the middle of the room. "And like I said, that ain't all. He's a buttboy, too."

"A buttboy. Cameron." It actually wasn't registering. "That means… what?"

"Dude, he gets fucked in the ass. He bends down, gets his butt up there, and they put it in. Gay boys are crazy for that shit. They dig Cam's ass, too. All macho and athletic. I'm tellin' you, he made some coin."

I was floored. A dude taking another dude's dick up is ass. Sucking another dude's cock. Letting him cum in your mouth, like some slutty girl. And not even 'cos you like it, but because they're paying you money. Not only did that seem fuckin' depraved to me, but Cameron was also a real stud-type and I never saw him going for that fag shit. The idea that he did it gave me total wood though. I asked Freddie how he knew about this and he told me Cam took him along a couple of times, and Freddie had sucked a few cocks.

"No shit, buddy," I guffawed, choking a little on my hit. "You crazy dude. What'd they pay you, man?"

Freddie shrugged. "I think I got a twenty off each of them. It weren't much. Bong money. You know." He smiled, all shy. "Didn't like it… well, nah, actually, weren't that bad." Then he took another toke, and then looked me in the eye with a stoned gaze. "But I'm tellin' ya, Cam man, he made the real dough. I admired that boy. I'd be just sucking off one guy, while he got off two or three with his ass. Paid him more, too."

The image of Cam's naked ass flashed before me. It was, by any objective measure, a real nice ass. Firm, curvy. Hard. Then I thought about cocks going in and out of it. And him liking it. Or, at least, enough to get paid. Not to mention Freddie, who was sitting right here. "And the, uh… sucking dick part, was that gnarly?"

"Nah," Freddie replied. "You can't be too uptight about it. But it's pretty easy, it's even kinda fun. You just put it in your mouth, keep your teeth outa the way, and try to do like girls all do for you." He smiled a bit as he smoked. "Cum tasted good, too. Gayboys pay for that. I still eat mine sometimes. I kinda miss the taste."

I laughed. "Crazy…" I said. But already the gears were turning in my head.

OK, here's where I come clean I guess. I like the ladies, but for a couple of months a few years ago my ass was the property of Jimmy Macon, an older kid at school. Call it curious teen experimentation, I guess. He was a hot property, real quarterback type, a jock among jocks. We met out at the quarry to get baked, and one time he sucked my cock. I fuckin' loved it but I said there was no way I was doing that for him. So he told me fine, I could take mine up the ass. For some reason that didn't sound as bad as giving a blowjob, so like an idiot I let him do it. I walked sideways for a week. But he did it again after that, and I liked it. He had a big dick and it just felt awesome inside me, stuffing my ass. When he came in me I felt like a girl.

I wasn't gonna tell Freddie all this, but I was way stoned, so I guess it all just poured out. At the end of my description he was looking at me in an odd way. Not mad, not laughing, just stoned I suppose, and also like, why the fuck did you just tell me all that, dude? But he was cool about it overall. He even asked some questions about it, how it felt and so on. I think he was curious, or maybe even a little turned on. I dunno.

Then he said: "Thing is, dude, you're a goodlooking guy. I'm really not into it, normally, but I know you could make some bank on this deal. I say you go for it. You know, you do got a pretty fuckin' amazing ass."

I knew that I did. That's why Jimmy singled me out, or so he'd said. I'm kind of short but I've got a rockin' little body, and I'm known as a fairly goodlooking guy. My ass makes a perfect, hard bubble in my jeans.

For the next day or two I kept thinking about it. Finally I decided to give Cameron a call.

––––––––––

"OK, rule number one is, get the money up front," Cam told me. We were in the dining hall of his dorm, which was a whole fuckin' lot nicer than the shithole where I still lived. I was eating a burrito. He had a bowl of Cap'n Crunch and like fourteen of those little cartons of milk. "Ain't nothin worse than bending over to take a dude's load up your ass, and then when you hit him up for the cash-ola he comes up short."

While he was talking I got distracted by his broad shoulders. He's a real stud of a guy, like I said. Solid body, hot chest, big fuckin' guns, and a nice, tightly-packed little ass, like mine I guess only Cam's taller. I remember being at a party once at some frat guys' house off-campus and I walked in on Cam fucking a girl. She was spread-eagle on the bed, moaning like girls do, her big perky tits bouncing around as he slammed into her. But what I really remember, before I shut the door again, was Cam's naturally muscular ass going up and down, rapid fire, his glute muscles making little dents in the perfect hairy globes of his cheeks.

I started going a little out of focus, thinking about this memory, and connecting it to the total dude's dude sitting across from me, telling me how he gets that same ass fucked. I suddenly wanted to see his ass again, for some reason. It almost made sense to ask him to show it to me. Then, I slowly came back to reality.

Cam continued the lesson. I looked in his brown eyes and tried to pay attention to what he was telling me.

"Make sure you tell him the first time he calls you how much all this shit is going to cost. That way he don't have no excuses when you show up at his door. I used to play all coy, but anymore dude I'm like a fuckin' streetwalker with that shit. Show me some interest and I can rattle off my whole price list, just like that."

I suddenly wondered if I should be taking notes.

"Rule number two," he went on. "Don't stick around. Half these gayboys, once they cum they get all mushy with ya. It's like a girl. They all wanna talk, talk, talk. Other day this kid asked me out to a movie with him, like, thirty seconds after he shot his load in my ass. A fuckin' movie." He rolled his eyes. "And then there's the ones who aren't gay, or don't think they are, or whatever. Who even fuckin' knows what they wanna talk about after, but they do. I just wear clothes that are real easy and fast to put back on once the deed is done."

"Uh huh," I nodded, blinking a little. I struggled to focus on these reminders, but I was still trying to picture Cam assuming the position. Did he bend over to get fucked by these guys? Or did he take it on his back, like I usually did with Jimmy Macon? His legs around their chests? "So, you're, uh… still doing it, then?"

"Fuck yeah," he said with his mouth wide open and full of cereal. "There's lots of demand around here, buddy, lots of gay dudes or bi dudes with extra cash left over after their beer allowances from mom and dad. It's a total buttboy's market around these parts." He paused to chew and swallow. "'Sides…" he added, a bit softer now, almost sheepish. "It ain't bad work. I kinda started to really like it after a while. Still do."

He let that hang in the air for a moment, kind of awkward but I was picturing him liking it, taking a hard dick up his ass, smiling and begging while some young dude blasted off in his hole, and I totally felt myself getting hard. I was wearing sweats with no jock, just boxers, so my fuckin' salami actually picked its whole self up off my right leg and started growing like a fuckin' redwood into the valley between my hairy thighs.

"Which brings me to rule number three," he said.

"What's that."

Cam flashed a huge grin, and reached over to grab me gently by the side of the neck. A fraternal gesture. "Have fun, man. You're out there getting paid, but man, let me tell ya—you're gonna wind up in some pretty hot and wild situations. Just go with it. College years are all about taking it easy and trying out new shit."

You know, I had to take his word on that one. So far I'd just been working my ass off just to make the grades and stay in the game here. Now, with this shit with Susie, I was all stressed out all the time because on top of everything, I had to make some more money. Other than drinking some on week-ends and toking up regularly with Freddie, I'd barely had fun that year at all. So, I decided to take Cam's advice to heart.

I was nervous as hell about my first pickup. I didn't want to move in on Cameron's territory—he was still working for the same boys who fucked him last year, most of whom now lived in his building or one of the other sophomore dorms nearby. So, stuck like I was in the freshman dorm, I figured I'd make the best of it and see if I could find any young johns among the incoming class. The problem was, how to get started?

"Let me get this right," Freddie said while we were smoking a few nights later. "You need, like, some kind of marketing plan for how to get some of these skinny little freshman dorks in this fuckin' skankhole where we're living to fuck your ass for money? Is that it?"

"Yeah, that's about it," I replied. "Hey, it was your idea, man. Any thoughts about how I get started?"

Fred let out a long whistle. "Not really, I guess. What I'm more worried about is, say you get one on the hook—how do you know you can do it?"

"Fuck that. I ain't gonna lose my nerve." That's one thing about me, when I say I'll do it, I follow through.

"No, that ain't it, buddy. I'm talking physically. You know, I give Tonya anal all the time, but it took like the first month before she could really fit me in. And I'm pretty fuckin' average down there, ya know."

I shrugged. "Like I said. The dude Jimmy in high school was hung like a motherfucker. And I took his fuckin' cock once, twice, up to three times or more a day. I was a total whore for him. And every time he wanted in me, he just slid right in, no problems. My ass was like a girl's pussy there toward the end of it."

"Right, but that was what, two years back? More?" He blew some smoke, and I thought about it. He was right, I might need to work up to it again. "Even pussies get tight if they don't get used for a while."

"So what, then. Get a dildo? I mean, I…put my finger in there, you know, sometimes, when I'm…ya know."

"Yeah yeah yeah, we all do that shit. But a finger and a dick are two different things, my man." He was suddenly speaking with some kind of authority, like he'd definitely given it some thought. I flashed back to the wild look he gave me when I first told him my high school story the week-end before. Now I seriously wondered if Freddie was going to come on to me, in some way. He was an alright looking guy, your basic shaggy-haired stoner dude but with a decent body and great skin. But he was my friend, and it was weird.

"Uh, you sayin'…? What?" I let the question hang in the air, un-asked. I also fingered my crotch a little bit.

Finally, reading my thoughts, Freddie let out a chuckle and reached over to his desk for the bag of weed. "OK, OK, buddy. This is a one-time offer. But I think I'm up for it. I just need some more of this stuff."

I thought about it for two more seconds and then grinned, a real shit-eater. Yeah, Freddie was a true friend. He refilled the bong, we both took some hits in silence, and then I could tell we were both ready to go.

I pulled my sweats off, giving me full mobility on my lower half, and hiked the old football jersey I was wearing part-way up my chest and back. Then I got on his bed where we'd been sitting, got in position on all fours, and pushed my ass up a little bit—just like I used to do for Jimmy Macon. At the memory of him fucking me so hard and so regular those few years before, I instantly grew a big hard-on, which I tried to hide from Freddie, but I'm sure he saw it. As Fred pulled his jeans off, he had the start of one of his own.

Naked, he looked at me on the bed, and shook his head one last time with nervous disbelief. Like, life is so fuckin' strange…what am I really doing here? But a second later he stepped over to me, and we got started.

First thing I saw was his half-hard dick in front of me, right at eye level. This was no accident, I knew. Fred talked constantly about how getting head was his number one thing to live for. He chose his girl, Tonya, because he said she gave the best, sluttiest blowjobs of any girl he'd met on campus. (To be fair, I think he'd met a total of three.) He kind of wagged it at me, and I licked my lips, but I was too shy to go any further.

"Dude, what gives," he said. "Think your boys ain't gonna want a little knob action before the main event?"

Truth was, I'd been reluctant to suck off Jimmy that first time at the quarry, but a week later I was doing it anyway. And soon after that, I was totally loving it. He gave me lots of pointers about it—I was younger, remember, and I'd only had one blowjob myself at that age, from a girl. By the end Jimmy told me I was pretty good. Now I'd find out, I guess. I took Freddie in my right hand and guided his skinny tool in my mouth. I closed my lips on his shaft, then went all the way down, and back up, once. Then I did it again, faster. Come to find out, it was like riding a bike. And I could tell right away that Freddie loved it too.

"Fu-u-uu-uck-kk…" he moaned. By instinct he put his hand on the back of my head and sort of massaged my buzzcut, pulling me harder onto his dick. That sort of pushed my slutty switch and I got all porno on him, deep throating that fucker, waxing it with spit, turning my mouth into a pussy for his hot raging bone.

After a few minutes, he reluctantly pushed me back. "Jesus dude," he panted. "You're fuckin' awesome at that shit. I'm totally gonna blast in a sec, so if you still wanna try it up your asshole you better do it now."

No worries. I flicked his lollipop dick one final time with my tongue, then re-assumed the position on the bed. Leaning forward and reaching back, I spat on my hand and worked the spit into my hole, pulling my cheeks apart to get them ready for their first splitting in over two years. I bet my ass looked fine like that, all hiked up and firm and ready for fucking. This was the asset I was planning on marketing, after all. I hoped it looked like the perfect thing that horny gay dudes would want to just stick their cocks in and fuck like hell.

Freddie climbed on the bed behind me, lined up his rod with my butt pucker, and then popped the head right inside. I jumped a little—shit, maybe he was right, and this would hurt like a motherfucker after all this time of not gettin' it. But I held strong. I turned my head toward him and nodded, a sign that he should start pushing the whole thing into me. And he did. I was afraid it would sting, and it did. But I got by with a lot of deep breaths, and by the time he rested against my lower back, with his whole cock bottomed out inside me, it was starting to feel OK. Then he took his first stroke out and back in, and I yelped again—only this time it was out of total pleasure. I had forgotten how fuckin' exciting it is to feel a dude's bone sink itself inside your ass, pull back, and then slam in deep once again. I fuckin' loved it, and told him to do it hard.

"You say so, boss," he quipped, and we were off.

Freddie really laid into my ass. I was glad he wasn't gentle. Gentle is for sissies. Jimmy never fucked me gentle. I knew some of these fags I'd be fucking would probably do me gentle, so that's cool, but really, if you're a man takin' another man's dick in you, all that sissy crap is really beside the point. You get fucked because you want to be fucked, so just take it. In fact, I figure you ought to be begging for it good and hard.

He railed my ass until I lost my balance, and my elbows splayed to the sides, pressing my chest down to the mattress and hiking my ass up even higher in the dorm room air. I do like taking it this way, because it helps both me and the dude fucking me appreciate the shape of my body. My ass sticking up looks fuckin' sweet. My chest muscles make a perfect cushion against the bed, bouncing me up and down with each deep fuck stroke that the dude throws into me from behind. Even my hot legs flex and tense from all the rhythm.

It wasn't very long before Freddie let out a kind of strangled yell, and I felt his boy cream ooze all over in my hole. Fuckin' hot. I loved getting spermed—I'd almost forgotten it, but it was what I looked forward to the most all those times when Jimmy and I would get together. I'd suck his rod, and take his bone up my ass, but the best feeling of all was when he squirted his flaming jock load way up deep inside me. And from what I could tell, Freddie was storing up just as much as Jimmy's biggest explosions—maybe more. He seemed to spray like a dozen times in me, and when he was done he stayed hard and fucked me some more.

All in all I think we were naked together for like an hour and half. That was a lot longer than I'd ever gone with Jimmy, because we were always sneaking our fucks in between classes or in one of our bedrooms back at home. Now, at college, and living alone, I realized that guys like Freddie and me (and Cam, who also had his own single) could get a lot more privacy when we needed it, and for longer stretches of time. The session with Freddie was a lot longer than Cameron had advised me to ever spend with my freshmen tricks, of course, but I didn't care—Fred and I were both horned, and I needed the practice and experience.

By the end of it Freddie got off three times up my ass. The only break we took was after his second load, when he fired up the bong and we took some more hits. We didn't talk at all while we smoked, and we both stayed naked, so I secretly hoped he'd be good for one more round. Sure enough, when the weed was gone again he threw me on my back and stood between my legs at the bed's edge, thrust his sore hard cock in my hungry little hole, and fuckin' rammed my ass like a maniac once more. In this position I could see his face, which was both weird and kind of cool. I mean, he was a friend who was now also a sexual buddy. And he looked pretty good like that, his face all intense and his biceps popping as he held my legs to each side and banged my butt. I wanted his third load so bad I started moaning and crying like a bitch. When he blasted it in me, I swear it was big as the first one. As he pulled out, all his cum sort of dribbled out around my hole.

"Oh dude..." he groaned finally, and a moment later he let out an exhausted laugh. "Un-fucking-believable. That was so fuckin' hot." He struggled to catch his breath. "You're gonna be popular at this, that's for sure."

"Yeah?" I asked, teasing his half-deflated cock by pushing my ass down toward it again. "I pass the test?"

Half-hearted, he pressed his cock against my hole and managed to get the head back inside me. All the spent jizz pouring out gave him enough lube to stick it back in an inch or so soft. Just that little bit in me felt fuckin' great. Feeling playful, I used my ass control to pinch his sensitive tip a couple of times.

"Ow," he said, sneering but with a smile. "Knock it off, ya fuckin' hussy. That's all I got."

(2)

SCALE

The next step was to do a little marketing. I knew which guys on my floor were gay, and I'd noticed some others in the building who were constantly checking me out, but I really had zero clue how to react to that. I mean, I'm not gonna flirt with fags. Being open about this shit is just not in the cards for me. It's gotta all be about discretion. If I could find some way to make myself available to them, without a direct confrontation, then I would be set. Once again, I deferred to my stud-whore-mentor, Cameron, for his advice in this area.

"What I did to get started," he told me, "was I put a little ad up on the main BBS. Nothing blatant, no pics or anything. There's codes you can use to say that you want some money. And then you leave it open about the kind of shit you'll do or you want them to do. Put it up there, keep cycling it, and see who responds."

I liked this approach—it was a way to take it slow at first, and see who responded. I made up an ad that was short and kind of vague, but that promised hot sex with a hot jock-type in exchange for time spent with a "generous" college-aged friend. I didn't list my exact location but narrowed it down to our campus. And I changed my age to be one year younger, hoping this would get more of the local freshmen to respond.

Holy man alive, did I get an avalanche of replies. At first I thought something was wrong with my inbox when the page took over a minute to load. In the first couple hours there were over fifty replies, and most of them had attached pictures. Lots of them were older, and a few sounded like total freaks. But after I read them all I had a list of about twelve or so that seemed like possibilities.

Over and over, they asked the same questions: What was I into, and how "generous" did they have to be?

I thought over Cam's advice, which was to be totally up front about the money thing in order to ward off future weirdness or surprises. I also remembered some marketing wisdom from a business class I'd taken the previous semester: Keep your message simple, and keep your cost of entry low. Somehow, forty dollars came to me as the perfect figure. I knew Cam charged more, but what the hell, I'm new at this. I figured I could always raise prices later, and if I dug getting fucked this much, I'd benefit from an economy of scale.

So, I phrased a one-line response and sent it to all twelve guys:

"Fuck me, dump your load in my jock ass. Two Jacksons. Campus only, your room. Discretion required."

———

Right, that did it. The first kid was Tommy Malone, this nerdy dude with braces (yeah, braces) who I'd met a couple of times in the laundry room.

I knew it would be him from his picture, and I was glad my first time out was someone I actually knew. He seemed like a nice kid. I never sent a face pic, though, so he didn't know it was me until I knocked on his door. His eyes got big and I could tell he was pretty happy about it.

Tommy knew next to nothing about what we were getting into, so I pretended like I knew everything. "You got something for me, man," I asked, and he pulled two twenties off the dresser and handed them over. Then I said, as businesslike as I could, "Right, so I'm gonna suck your cock for a little bit, and when you're ready, I'm gonna let you fuck my ass. When you fuck me, you gotta keep going 'til I get your load. Cool?"

He just nodded. I dropped down on my knees, unzipped him, and started fishing through his tighty-whities to get at his bone. It was long and skinny, smelled kinda funky but in a nice way. He was standing in the middle of the room, so when I first took him in my mouth, he was overwhelmed and started to lose his balance. I pulled off his cock and led him over a few steps to the bed, staying on my knees. Once he sat on the mattress I was more free to really give him some intense head—you know, the good slutty kind, lots of spit, lots of tongue, lots of fast and slow strokes. Tommy dug it but he was ready to cum almost right away.

"I…I'm gonna…" he started to say.

Unfortunately I didn't figure him out right away, and a few seconds later his cum blasted all over in my mouth. It scared the shit out of me, not because I didn't like it, but because it wasn't part of my master plan.

"Shit!" I pulled off him quickly, his first few shots pouring off my lips, and his skinny wang still spasming all over. I was pissed that it happened, but come on, I'm never going to begrudge another dude his orgasm. So I kept pulling on Tommy's cock until the moment started to pass, and then I sucked him back in once again to eat his load and get him cleaned up. His cum was only the second dude's I'd ever tasted in my life.

Then there was this awkward pause. He looked down at me, like, what now? I could tell he still wanted to fuck me. I'd been in that room for less than one minute. He still had all his fuckin' clothes on, for chrissake.

Finally, on my knees, still pulling on his cock, I looked up with my cum-covered face and told him: "If you still wanna fuck me Tommy, let's do it. But it's gonna be another forty bucks." That only seemed fair to me.

His expression changed to such sadness I thought he was going to cry. "I ain't got it right now," he said.

I stood, smiling. "It's cool. Well, let me know when you do." I grabbed some tissues from the box on his crappy little desk, and used them to wipe off my face and chin. "Later, man." Then I went out the door.

Back in the hallway, two floors below my own dorm room, I took a gulp of breath. My heart was racing a bit, and it suddenly occurred to me that it might look odd for me to be leaving this freshman kid's room. For future jobs, I would make sure the john checked the hallway for me first, to make sure the coast was clear. But this time, I was lucky…not a soul in sight. I took a deep breath, and relaxed a bit. I had just made forty bucks for a few minutes of work. And I liked it. This was going to be great. Still, I had to play it cool.

When I got back to my room and sat at my computer, I realized two things. First of all, I had seven more guys who were definitely on for meeting with me, and based on how things had just gone with Tommy, it would be no problem to get with all seven of them yet tonight. That's how I was going to make my cash at this thing, I reminded myself— economies of scale. Forty bucks was nothing to pay for good sex, no matter how quick it was, so I simply had to get my name out there and get some regular customers to fill my time.

The other thing I realized—speaking of filling things—was that my ass was twitching. Unconsciously, I had been looking forward to getting fucked, and now that I was back in my room without having even taken my jeans off, my ass was letting me know how disappointed it felt that it didn't get any action. This surprised me, but then, this whole thing was kinda a big revelation for me. Cam said to enjoy it, and I guess I did.

The next guy wasn't anyone I recognized. He looked way arty, like some kind of geeky emo boy—thin face, longish stringy bangs, and skinny legs, though he swung a pretty good package of meat from the X pic he sent me. Checking again, I saw that he lived on my floor. The dorm was huge, so it wasn't surprising that I didn't recognize him, but I doubted I'd even seen him before. I had no idea who he was at all. Oh well.

We traded IMs, and twenty minutes later I was knocking on his door. When he let me in, I saw the room was dim with some candles, and there was a stick of some crazy smelling shit on fire in the corner— incense, I guess. Whatever. I thought about Cam's warning that some of the fagboys like to make this all romantic and whatnot. I could go along with that, as long as we finished up on time and they had the money to pay.

He was pretty cool. I never got his name, but when I said I'd never met him, he said he was an architecture student. I guess they pretty much live down in the studio 24/7, even freshman year. He told me he'd seen me around and was pretty glad I turned out to be who I was. He didn't seem nervous at all. This one totally had his shit together, it seemed. He probably had some decent experience, too. This put me more at ease.

"Forty, right," he asked, going through his wallet. I didn't say anything. The rules, Cam told me, are that they've got to specifically offer the money before you say anything about it. So when the kid flashed two bills at me a moment later, I just grunted and nodded, and then I tucked them in my pocket. We were off.

To my surprise, his next move was to step in and try to kiss me. I backed off, muttering, "Uh…I don't…"

He didn't protest, but he seemed a little peeved. "OK, whatever. Sex without kissing is just weird for me."

I didn't know what to say, and I thought it might be over. I briefly wondered if I should give the money back, but that seemed stupid. Luckily, we were still on. He stepped back, unzipped himself, pulled his jeans down to his ankles, and then lay back on his dorm cot and spread his sexy legs wide. "Go nuts," he told me.

Seconds later I was sucking my second cock of the night. I tried to go a little slower and less Monica this time, in case he was a hair trigger like the previous kid. But he seemed OK with the pace, and he had a great cock for sucking, so I just relaxed there on my knees and gave it some time. By the point where he wanted to move things along, I actually felt like I wanted the blowjob to continue for a while longer.

Still, business is business. I stood up, pulled my shirt off, and unbuttoned the top button on my jeans. I knew I looked good like this, so I decided to stand there a second and kind of show off. The kid approved.

"Right," I said finally. "So, kid. How do you wanna fuck me?"

He was smiling up at me, kind of girlish, pulling on his cock. "You sure you don't wanna fuck me?"

Ha. Yeah, I knew I'd get this from the fagboys. I had to be strict. "My ad was pretty clear," I said evenly.

"Right." He got the picture. "OK, get down here on your back. Legs up. I wanna see you that way."

I pulled my jeans and boxers off, giving him a bit more of a show, and then followed his directions. He moved aside so I could stretch out on the thin bed. Once I got in a comfortable position, I bent my legs and raised them up a little bit, kind of suggestively. The kid looked on, still beating off, but he didn't move to touch me. So I played with my own cock a bit, which was gettin' chubby. I dug this scene. After a few strokes I reached down with my free hand to play with my ass, which was still twitching from craving cock.

When I did this, the kid practically started purring. "Yeah…" he moaned. "Big fuckin' jock. You wanna take it…" He stroked slowly on his cock, which by now was dripping precum all over his hand. He looked hot.

"Do it, man," I said, trying to sound commanding but it came out sorta like a beg. "Yah, I need it… fuck me."

Gradually, the kid moved further onto the bed, and by the time I felt him gently raising my legs up, my cock reached its full hard-on and my legs took over on their own, hoisting up high to let this big-dicked john in to have his way with me. He lined up his cock with my ass, and after some slight jockeying back and forth around my hole, he poked the head in, then slid his whole nine inches all the way in, like butter.

Holy shit, it felt great. This was a bigger cock than Freddie had fucked me with—maybe even as big as Jimmy, all those years before. And the kid knew how to use it. From the first few seconds I was whining and moaning like a little fuckin' girl. It just felt so fuckin' sweet. He fucked me steadily but gently at first, and then before long he picked up the pace a bit. I felt an instinct to reach out and grab him, not to kiss him or any shit like that, but just so I could hang on. I grabbed the cloth T-shirt over his bony little shoulders (he was still dressed—his jeans were even still around his ankles) and pulled him into me with every deep stroke. By the end of it he was long-dicking my hole and I was whooping so loud I thought the whole dorm could hear me. When he sprayed his load in me my own cock shot off all over my hairy, muscular chest.

We pulled apart, panting, not talking. I wanted to say: Jesus fucking christ, that's hot. But I played it cool.

Instead, I just got dressed, and said: "We can do it any time. I'm just down the hall, man. Let me know."

Four out of the five guys remaining on the list ended up meeting with me that night. Two of them couldn't ditch their roommates and wanted to each come by my room, so I said that was OK. They turned out to be the hottest sex of the whole night…jocks like me, totally on the down low, with awesome little bodies and nice fat dicks. Their names were Ike and Reed. They each arrived separately, fucked my ass but hard, and promptly left again after spewing their seed in my hole. What I really wanted was to get them both to come back sometime together. But they were closet cases, I could tell, so that suggestion probably wasn't cool.

The other two were more or less like the first guy, Tommy, nervous little nellies who all the same paid me in advance with a minimum of bullshit, and unlike Tommy, actually took their chance to throw a nice mean fuck into my cummy hole. (I tried cleaning up between sessions, but the reality was that having a bit of nature's lube up there was helpful when you're doing multiples in one evening…another tip I'd gotten from Cameron.) Both guys also seemed cool about keeping things discreet, so I told them to e-mail me anytime.

The next day over a mid-afternoon bong, Freddie was all eager to get details. "Tell me about it, stud," he said. "How'd your first night go? You get some of those cute little freshman dickies to squirt in your hole?"

"Fuckin' right. And I got three hundred bones to show for it." I wasn't gonna let Freddie tease me about this when the whole thing was his suggestion.

Even stoned, it didn't take Fred long to do the math. "You got fucked seven times?" He appeared shocked.

"Six," I said. "First dude came in my mouth. Whoops." I took a toke. "And I even got an extra twenty from this jock. You shoulda seen it—he was there at my room, and this other jock was there, like, a half-hour later. I bet they totally know each other. And they had a pretty good time. I'll be hearing from them again."

Freddie was still dealing with the reality that I'd been fucked multiple times. "Cam never took that many at once. I don't think, at least. Six cocks? Up your ass? Dude, how is that even possible? Your ass should be, like, broken by now."

Inside my sweats, as a reflex, I clenched my ass for a second. It still felt tight, and still had some jizz in it.

"Nah." I shrugged. "I guess it's a lot. But I took it like a champ, man. It was fuckin' hot. Plus, I let each guy shoot his cum inside there, and that ends up lubing me for the next dude, so each fuck gets a little easier."

Freddie thought about this, then shrugged also. "Guess that makes sense."

I didn't know how to tell him this, but my ass was twitching again. He'd shared with me earlier that his girl, Tonya, was being bitchy and not putting out the last few days. So I had an opening—Fred needed to get off.

"So," I said, casually as I could. "You got a load for me, big guy? Or did you already wank it away?"

He shot me a look. I couldn't tell if he was pissed. Then he asked, "Do I gotta pay you forty bucks?"

"Fuck that, dude," I said happily, getting my sweats off. "Just keep me in weed. You're cool."

The best part about this was that Freddie didn't even move. He was laid back on his bed, holding the bong. The TV was on in the corner, with the sound turned down really low. He half-watched the show while I pulled his pants open far enough to get at his cock. I blew him a little to get him hard, and then I squatted down over him, aiming his bone for my aching hole. Then I held onto this wall shelf above us for support, and by moving up and down I basically jerked him off with my ass. He watched TV, took a few more bong hits, and then after ten minutes or so I heard him gulp slightly, and he shot his big wad up into my asshole.

I climbed off of him. My ass was happy, for now. I'd try to get a few more loads for pay online that night.

"Fuckin' wild, dude," was all Freddie said, after I was fully dressed.

"Later man," I replied, grabbing a mint to hide my breath, and headed out the door to go back to my room.

"Six is a lot," Cameron was saying to me that night at dinner. "I'd take it easy tonight, dude. Your ass can stretch like that, especially when you're lubing it with loads, but it's not a good idea to take on so many all at once." We were having a quick meal. I hadn't planned on seeing him, but wanted to share my news.

"Right, OK," I agreed. "Uh…so, how many…dudes do you get with? Usually? In a week?"

He counted silently. "Usually about a dozen. Maybe more. I've got regulars, they've even got their own days of the week. But on weekends they can get real slutty. They bring their friends over, so that's more."

"No shit? Like how many dudes?"

"Most I've had so far is eight at a time, but there was one week-end a few months back where I got twenty dudes to fuck me in four different meet-ups," Cam replied. "I was a whore for all of them. They all came in me, both ends. I was like this little fuck doll, and they all fuckin' loved it. Reminded me of the slutty girls who show up at the frat house on Friday night and don't leave until their first class on Monday morning."

"Jesus," I said. "And you're sayin' I'm the one who should take it easy?"

Cam blushed. It was slightly cute. "Yeah, I know. I'm just saying, you gotta work your way up to that shit."

Later that day, when I was douching in the shower to get ready for the evening's action, I thought about slutty Cameron taking all those dicks in one week-end. Needless to say, I threw instant wood. How a stud like that could fly below the radar—woo the girls and be a total slamhound for the guys—it was a mystery to me. It was also a total turn-on, and an inspiration. I was popular with the ladies myself, but I knew how much I was starting to enjoy all of this male action my ass was getting. So if Cam could do it, so could I.

A couple of hours after that, I was on my back in some freshman's lower bunk, legs up. I hooked my toes around the metal slat that supported the upper bunk above me, and then spread my sexy legs wide to give the kid access. He was a homely dude, but he sported some giant wood. Like, the biggest one I've seen yet.

"You sure?" he asked softly. I guess he saw me admiring his hang. "I know I'm big."

"Fuckin' huge," I blurted out, but I was more excited than worried. "Go for it, man. I got a real easy hole."

And I was right…the kid slid right in, no problems. He seemed impressed, and so was I. For my first fuck of the night, I expected his monster cock to give me pain, and it did a little at first, but after that I just kicked back and took it. His huge log just sawed in and outa me, and I fuckin' loved it. All through dinner I craved getting stuffed by a big dick, and now I was getting my wish. Better yet, for the effort, I had two crisp bills in the pocket of my jeans, which right now were hanging over the back of this ugly hung kid's desk chair.

"Fuck me," I grunted, reaching around to clutch his fat ass cheeks and yank his dick deeper inside my guts. He took the cue and picked up the pace. I started groaning, real deep. It just felt too fuckin' good.

As I took his cock, I remembered another tip Cameron had told me about, which was to squeeze my ass a little bit each time the guy fucking me is sinking his cock up my ass. I remembered doing this for Jimmy too, driving him crazy, but I'd forgotten about the technique over the years. Cameron said he did it to make his johns cum faster, so he could get on his way, but I suspected he did it for another reason, also…the same reason I liked it: it turned the dude on more, and made him shoot his load deeper and harder up my ass.

I applied this advice to my current trick, and sure enough, right away he was gasping. I shut my eyes in anticipation of a nice, goopy teen load going straight up into my butt. Seconds later, that's just what I felt.

When he pulled out, I relaxed for a minute, catching my breath. My gaping butt hole took on a breeze from the room, like someone left a fuckin' window open. Jesus, that boy was huge. I hoped he'd be a regular.

I looked over at the kid, and he was on his cell phone. "You mind?" he said to me. "I got some buddies who wanna stop over."

Before I could answer, he was chatting with some other dude. Their conversation lasted just a few seconds, and when he hung up, we both stayed silent. I kept my legs where they were, spread and lifted, hooked on the upper bunk support. I stretched them a little, trying to relax. My first gangbang was only minutes away.

The guys must have lived real close by, because it was less than a minute later that I heard a knock at the door, and the kid who fucked me was letting three more guys into the room. All three of the guys were a lot cuter than the kid whose room we were in. Then I saw that one of them was Ike, one of the two hot jocks who fucked me the night before. He looked at me like he didn't recognize me. Guess he was playing it cool.

All three guys had no qualms about being there, or what they were there to do. Seeing a hot dude on the bed, pantsless, with his faded T-shirt pulled up over his neck, and his legs hoisted up and fresh cum leaking out of his asshole, didn't seem to phase these dudes in the least. Right away, they started getting undressed.

"Arright, let's do this," one of them said, this tall, tan dude with curly black hair.

"Right," I said. But business came first. "So...it's forty each. Put the money in my jeans pocket. Over there."

One by one, they shelled out the cash and tucked it into the pocket of my jeans, which were still on the desk chair. The last dude, a skate-rat type, paid with a whole pile of bills that didn't quite total forty bucks, so he had to bum the extra singles off one of his friends. When they'd all paid, they stepped over to the bed.

Skater boy stuck it to me first. He had a nice rod, not too big, but comfortable. I think he lasted about twelve seconds. I took his load, and I liked it. Then he moved aside, and the tall one stepped in. This kid threw one mean, serious fuck, but I totally liked that, too. Even better, while the tall dude was doing me, Ike the jock stood next to the bed and spanked his fat dick on my face a couple of times, telling me to suck. So I turned my neck and gave him a blowjob, while he rested his chest and arms on the upper bunk and just humped in and out of my mouth. It was a big fuckin' turn-on to suck his big dick, which had fucked me less than twenty-four hours earlier, while his buddy railed the shit out of me, right between my legs, on the bed.

When tall boy came, I expected Ike to take his turn, but instead the ugly kid got in there and worked his huge tool into me, wanting more. "Don't worry, I slipped ya another forty," he muttered, and then took off ramming me like a maniac. Jesus, it felt great. He must've been inspired by his tall friend's style because he totally tore my ass up. His cock was so big and thick it plunged all the other loads out of me with every stroke. He fucked me so hard and so good, I was practically crying while I tried to resume sucking off Ike.

Finally, ugly boy came in me, and I swear he shot as much as the first time. At this point I was slightly delirious from so much action. Only Ike remained to fuck me. I figured we were almost done, and I was right— but, instead of just fucking me like his buddies had, Ike had a few more tricks up his sleeve. First of all, when he got on the bed, I could see he was making his way down on me with his face, and I thought for a second he might give me a blowjob. My fat ol' dick had been rock hard since before these guys had even entered the room, so I was aching for release. Instead of blowing me, though, he totally surprised me by sticking his face deeper, and lining it up with my ass. I felt his tongue on my hole, which was oozing cum, and Ike started eagerly lapping my butthole and all the spent fuck-slime that was down there. Fuckin' nasty!

After rimming me and slurping those loads, Ike got up on his haunches and stuck himself in my slutty jock cunt. It felt better than ever. Then, while he was fucking me, he grabbed the dick of the ugly kid who was standing right next to him, gave it a few yanks, and then stuck it in his mouth. The ugly kid's giant hard-on was unstoppable. Ike did an impressive job of taking it deep in his mouth without losing the rhythm of deep-fucking my hot, sloppy ass. So I took his repetitive drilling, turned-on even more by the sight of him sucking that big cock while he fucked me. I was getting close to cumming, so I reached down for my dick and started to jerk myself off. When I saw the ugly kid's third load start spilling out over Ike's lips, I lost it.

Ike, the pro, realized I was cumming and timed himself to shoot off up my ass at the same time I was spraying my own load all over my ab muscles, chest, and neck. Jesus, what a nut. It was the best cum I think I had since I started college. And of course, bearing down on Ike's bone to shoot my load only made him shoot harder. His jock juice joined the other guys' jizz up in my hole. And when he pulled out, he stuck his cute cummy face down there again and eagerly drank up his own sauce where it poured outa my pucker.

––––––––––––

Counting my money back in the room, I realized what "economy of scale" really meant. I'd pulled in $200 in less than forty-five minutes. And I still had three more tricks scheduled for that night. Assuming each of them gave me forty bucks and a load, in less than two hours I'd have over three hundred bucks—the same amount as the previous night's earnings, in less than half the time—not to mention the awesome feeling of eight sweet cum loads from seven different guys swimming around in my tight jock belly. Life was good.

(3)

LIMITS

That second night, after taking all those cocks, including my first mini-gangbang, I had this wild dream. Cam was fucking me. He had this big ol' whopper of a dick. (I didn't know his actual cock size at the time. Turns out he is actually pretty big.) Anyway, just as he was loading his cream in me, I looked around, and saw there were all these other guys around us. Like, dozens of them. All college dudes, too. Some of them I recognized from living in our dorm last year. I figured out that these were all of the guys who had fucked Cameron's ass at one time or another. They totally filled the room where we were fucking, and spilled out the door into a hallway, where I could see there were a ton more. There was a window next to the bed, and outside I saw more and more guys, as far as the eye could see. There were hundreds of them altogether.

"All these guys fucked me," Cameron said, huffing and puffing as he shot his load up my ass. "They shot their cum in me. And now, I'm shooting all their cum into you. You've been a good student, Travis boy..."

That's when I realized that the cum he was shooting up my ass didn't seem to end. It just kept flowing and flowing. Thirty seconds, a minute, many minutes, a half hour...all the guys were hanging out and smiling and high-fiving each other as Cam shot gallon after gallon of cum up into my asshole with his huge dick.

In the dream, I had two reactions. One, I thought Cameron was a total stud for having such a big load to give me. Here I knew him as a total buttboy for pay, like I was, but it turned out he totally knew how to please my ass and give me tons and tons of manly seed. The other thing I figured out, though, was that even though he was shooting so much cum into me—thousands of loads, probably—and even though his cock was so fuckin' big, I would never be satisfied. By re-introducing me to man sex and re-training me on how to take cocks and loads inside me, he had ruined me for any other kind of sex, ever again. I was a slut now, in the truest sense: I got fucked because I needed it, and I let guys pay me money to do it. I was a total whore who needed more and more cocks and cum inside my ass. No amount of it would ever be enough.

Realizing this freaked me out, and I looked deep in Cameron's eyes as the never-ending cum geyser continued shooting into my hot ass like a fuckin' cannon. Cameron didn't say anything, but the look in his eyes said: It's cool, buddy. You're a hot dude, and you know how to take it. Own it. This is who you are.

I started to accept it then. This was who I was now. A slutty young dude on his back in some bed, his jock ass getting filled with so much cum that it kept running out all over the place. This was me, every day for the rest of my life, probably. It scared me to accept this, but it also made me feel peaceful. Then, I woke up.

"Congratulations," Cameron said over breakfast the next day. "Man, it was a few months before I got multiple action off the boys. Here, you go and do it your second time out." He seemed a little jealous.

"It was way hot," I said. "They totally knew what they were doing, too. I'm gonna learn a ton of new shit."

"Yeah, you will. For every newbie little twink who gets all nervous and fucks up, you're gonna get a kid who knows just what he wants, and pushes you until he gets it." Cam took another mouthful of cereal. "I remember the first time a kid sat on my face. I was like, what the fuck. I didn't know I was supposed to lick his asshole. Shit, I didn't even know that was something you can do. Finally he said, Lick it bitch, so I did."

"Yeah? See, I didn't even know that," I told him. "Although this one jock last night at the gangbang did something a little fuckin' depraved." I told him about Ike sticking his face down there and licking up the loads that he and the other dudes had shot in my ass. "He loved it, too. Went at it like it was his last meal."

Cam nodded. "It's called felching. Some guys are really into eating cum. They suck cock so they can eat your load, and when they fuck a load in your ass they eat it back out again. It's way sick, but it's kinda hot."

"Yeah, I know. Exactly."

He went on to describe some other fetishes he'd run across. He had one regular kid who got off on Cam's feet, and also his dirty socks. "I gotta keep a stash of socks in my room from when I get back from working out," he said. "I let 'em get crusty for a few days, then I bring 'em along when I go to this kid's room."

That sounded kinda odd. "And…he does, like, what with them?"

Cameron shrugged. "Rubs 'em around his face and his body, mostly. Sometimes he sticks a sock in his mouth while I'm blowing him or riding his cock. He tried sticking one in my mouth once while he was riding my ass doggy-style, but I wouldn't let him. I made it clear that wasn't my scene."

He then rattled off the other things that weren't his "scene" and by the end of it I'd pretty much lost my appetite for breakfast. I know I'm just a white trash punk from the cornfields, but I really had no fuckin' idea that some dudes got off on this shit. Like, literally shit, for example. Guys want you to shit on them and, fuck knows, rub it around, or whatever. Or they wanna piss in your mouth. Get with a dog. Shit like that. I was pretty disgusted, but I didn't say anything. There were probably guys who would be pretty disgusted by the shit me and Cam DID do for our tricks, so I guess I gotta say, to each his own. But still.

"So," Cam finished, "make sure you tell guys what your limits are. And that's today's lesson, buckaroo." He stuffed one last slice of cold toast in his mouth, grabbed his backpack, and headed out of the cafeteria.

Sure enough, that afternoon I get an e-mail response from my ad, saying: "What are your limits?"

I wrote back listing all the crazy shit Cameron had mentioned, saying don't even talk to me if you wanna do any of that. Then I tried to think of other stuff, but I really couldn't. In one other ad online, I'd seen a guy say: "No pain, no drugs" so I added that too. The dude replied saying that was all cool. He wanted to know, though, if I would be OK with getting blindfolded, and fucked by him and his roommate, while they got it on video. I thought about that one, and was getting hard, so I wrote back and said that would be OK.

Of course, a few hours later, when I was actually going to their room, I thought: What the fuck am I getting into? These guys could be total sadists and maniacs. I can defend myself against any one guy, but two guys might be a different story, especially if they've got me blindfolded or tied up in any way. I decided to call Cameron, just to let him know what I was doing, and to find out if he had any advice.

"Just the usual, bro," he said. "Trust your instincts and get the money up front. I think I know the two guys you're talking about. They go at it all intense, but they're pretty harmless. They actually like to make out the whole time they're doing you, which they're embarrassed about and that's one reason for the blindfolds."

I thanked him, and shut my cell phone. Making out, I thought. Huh. I thought about the kid that first night who tried kissing me. Then I was standing at the dorm room door, and with a burst of courage, I knocked.

The dude who opened the door was pretty scrawny, but in a cute way. He had a mellow smile and I could tell from the smell that he was getting high. He let me in, and I saw his roommate relaxed on the bed, also smiling and looking pretty baked. I realized immediately I had nothing to worry about. Two stoner closet cases couldn't cause me much trouble, even if I had one hand tied behind my back. Probably even two.

"You got something for me?" I asked.

"Fuck yeah," the dude on the bed said, approvingly. He was goodlooking, and he had a better body going on than his buddy. He looked like the basic boy next door. His jeans showed a good sized bulge. "Give our slut his money, man. I wanna get this started." The other dude took out four twenties and gave them to me.

I got undressed fast and got on the bed, next to the more built guy. I started playing with my cock, thinking about him kissing the other skinnier dude and I swear to god it got me hard. The skinny guy set up a little video camera in the corner, then grabbed a necktie from the top drawer of the dresser and tossed it over to me. Wordlessly, I wrapped it around my head and tied it in back, shutting out all the dim light of the room, leaving me in total darkness. Then, a second later, I heard him click the switch on the camera. We were off.

The dude on the bed started in on me right away, rubbing my chest and arms hard with his big warm hands. I've got some solid guns and pecs, and they look good with my pure skin, so I knew he was digging it. Me, I felt really fuckin' excited as well. I continued touching my dick for a while but then I backed off, enjoying the massage. As soon as my hand moved away I felt a warm mouth go on my cock and I realized the skinny dude was giving me head. Eventually the built dude crawled on top of me and straddled my chest, rubbing my strong pec and ab muscles over and over. I'd spent an hour and a half in the weight room that afternoon, working my upper body, so his touch felt fantastic, and he seemed like he was really into doing it to me.

A buckle snapped near my face, but both hands stayed on me, so I figured out the skinny guy was undoing the built guy's jeans. He seemed to tug them down a little bit, and then his mouth left my cock. The licking sounds I heard a moment later, following by moans from the dude giving me the massage, made me realize that skinny boy had his tongue up the other stud's ass and was rimming him nice and deep. Skinny was still between my legs, and after a minute or two I started wondering if he'd give my ass the same treatment. So like the horny little ass-whore I had now become, I spread my legs wide and lifted them up a bit, onto the skinny guy's shoulders. I did this in the total blackness of my blindfolded state, making it even more unreal.

Built guy figured it out right away. "Lick his ass, man," he said, kind of gentle but also commanding. His voice sounded sexy as hell, even more so because he was so close to me and yet I couldn't see him. Sure enough, a moment later there was that sweet little lapping at my boy hole that I'd felt for the first time the day before, when Ike had gone there to felch out those gangbang loads. Following that 4-on-1 fuck session, I had proceeded to get fucked six more times that evening, all one-on-one encounters, each resulting in a big load getting sprayed up in my sweet round butt. I had cleaned up totally for this session, but I wondered if maybe even some of the cum from the previous day's customers might still be dripping out of my hole, where the skinny kid was sliding his long tongue in and out. I secretly hoped he was getting a taste.

My massage from the built dude continued a little while, and I was in bliss from all the attention my sore muscles and hungry ass were receiving from these boys. Then the dude on top of me crawled off, saying: "Alright, move over. I gotta fuck this sweet slut's hole." The skinny dude's rim job must have prepared me well, because I could tell that the cock going into me a few seconds later was one of the biggest I'd taken so far. I howled happily as this little hunk filled my ass with his big rod, and then started pushing it in and out.

"Fuck yes," the dude inside me sputtered. "Holy fuck...fuck, this is a sweet fuckin' hole. Fuckin' perfect."

While he banged me hard, I heard the skinny dude come around to the side of the bed, and then the mattress got pushed down slightly right next to my neck. Then my lips were slapped a couple of times by what I realized had to be the tip and shaft of the skinny dude's dick. In a low voice, he said simply: "Suck."

I opened my mouth wide and started giving him head. It was kind of a struggle in this position, but I made it work. He had a nice long pole, not too thick or anything so I was able to slide it down my throat pretty far. Meanwhile, his buddy continued packing my ass deep and hard. My raging boner bounced against my hard belly over and over. In the blackness, I pictured how the three of us looked from above: Me, spread eagle and getting fucked like the cheap hooker I was, my legs up on this sexy freshman's shoulders while his skinny roommate face fucked me, making me slobber all over my own chin, dampening the blindfold.

It was hard work, but like I said before, when I commit to something, I just fuckin' do it. This was my job now, taking dick at both ends, doing whatever I had to in order to make these dudes happy so they'd get their money's worth and keep inviting me back. I was totally theirs for pleasure. Within the professional limits that I established, they could feel free to do with me whatever they want. I grunted as the skinny dude's cock pushed in and out of my face in long swipes, meanwhile clenching my hole on my fucker's thick sexy dick.

Built dude spewed in my hole, which felt fuckin' awesome. And he finished it just right, pulling out and letting his cum ooze out just a little before his roomie joined in. Then I took the same kind of deep fucking from the skinny kid, while the built hunk took his place next to my face and force-fed me his spent cock to lick and suck clean. The flavor of his cum and my ass that I sucked off his dick was pretty fuckin' nice.

Turns out the skinny kid wanted to really rail my ass like a bucking bronco, so eventually they both pulled out of me and had me spin over on my knees. Then skinny dude sunk his long rod in me again, and fucked the holy hell out of me for another ten straight minutes before his hot teenage goo finally shot up in my ass.

They let me rest for a minute, and then I took the blindfold off. They'd both put their boxers back on by that point, and the skinny one had stopped the camera. I started gathering my own clothes, ready to take off. Out of the corner of my eye I noticed that both guys' boxers showed they were still plenty hard. I half-wondered what kind of special video-viewing party they had in mind after they showed me out and shut the door.

The built guy, who I realized now had a lightly hairy chest and looked fuckin' hot in his underwear, gave his whopper a little extra tug through the boxers fabric, and started in with some conversation. "So what's your name, man. You were fuckin' great and we wanna do all that to your hot ass again sometime."

"Travis," I said. "Anytime."

"I'm Dexter. This is Les," he said, gesturing to the skinny one.

I nodded politely to both guys. "Cool. It was really hot. Just text me or e-mail me whenever you want it."

When I left their room and got to the lobby, I had a few minutes to wait for the elevator, and my eyes happened to fall on a sign-up sheet for some kind of dorm floor event. Bored, I decided to scan the sheet for the names of the guys who'd just fucked me. I saw Dexter toward the top of the list. Room 512. Then a ways down I saw Les. Room 512 also. Something seemed odd. I looked at Dexter again, and then it hit me. Both guys had the same last name. And it was a pretty unusual name, not like Smith or whatever. Brothers!

"They're fuckin brothers, dude," I said to Cameron when I called him a fucking split-second later. He was laughing at the other end. "You fuckin' set me up to get fucked by two fuckin' brothers. Fuckin' twisted."

"Yeah, I guess," Cam said. "One's actually a year older than the other one, but they both ended up at the same school. Figure that one out. And I guess they also wanted to, uh, live together… for some reason…"

"Jesus Christ. Yeah, I wonder what fuckin' reason that might be. What a couple a fuckin' pervs."

"Ah come on," he said. "Keep your mind open, little grasshopper. Don't judge their little special happiness. Besides, it's just fucking. A hole is a hole, bro. You telling me you never shared pussy with another dude?"

"All the fuckin' time, man, but just not with my fuckin' brother!" Actually, I didn't have a brother, but still.

There was a pause. Cameron laughed again, but said nothing. Then I remembered what he said earlier.

"Wait, and they make out together? Is that what you told me? As in, they, like, kiss each other and shit?"

"Oh yeah, big time. I'm not shitting you. They gave me one of the videos they made of me getting railed. They were fuckin' all over each other. They mack on each other the whole time they're doing me at both ends.

At the end of the video, after I split, they even suck each other off and cum on each other's faces."

I let out a long sigh. Here I'd been thinking all day about my limits. Never fuckin' thought about this.

"Fuckin' pervs," was all I could say, and then I hung up.

But of course, two images stuck in my mind for hours after that. First, the brothers making out. For some reason that gave me a total boner. I was actually getting mighty curious at this point, I'll admit, what kissing a dude might be like. Or at least watch two guys do it. Second, I couldn't shake the image of both brothers fucking Cam. While he's blindfolded. I pictured the cocky smile on Dexter's face while he pulled on his cock and watched his skinny little brother putting his own schlong all the way up Cameron's sweet, hot ass.

I thought about it the rest of the evening, all through getting fucked by my remaining three tricks of the night. As I walked back from the final encounter, sticking the bills in my jeans pocket, I realized that my hard-on had not gone down. I was glad when I got to the room and Freddie wasn't around to bug me, because I ripped open my fly and just stood there in the middle of my dorm room, beating off to the image of the brothers kissing while they tag-teamed Cam's ass. Blindfolded. Over and over. While making out.

In under thirty seconds I shot a giant load all over the dorm room floor.

"Alright, so I totally gotta see that video now, dude," I shyly confessed to Cam the next morning in the cafeteria. "You put that image in my fuckin' head, and I gotta see it for myself."

"Video?" He played dumb. "The one where the brothers fuck you? Ask them yourself. I don't have it."

"No, idiot, the video they gave you. Where they fuck you."

He looked at me wide-eyed, then slowly smiled. "Dude, you want to see video of me getting fucked?"

I could feel myself blushing. "And the brothers…you know…mackin' on each other. I gotta see this."

He teased me about it for the rest of the meal, until I finally told him to fuckin' forget it, and I left.

Still, two days later, back at the cafeteria again, Cam slipped me the disc. I said thanks, and went directly up to my empty room and didn't leave for two hours, during which time I think I shot four fuckin' loads.

Back at my computer, I thought about updating my ad to say "No brother sex" but that seemed like a pretty weird thing to say all on its own. So I didn't change it. Then I pondered the obvious question: Now what? What happens when Dexter or Les tried to contact me again? Do I come clean that I know their little secret, or do I play along like they're just two buds looking for an anonymous hole to tag-fuck whenever they get horny? And the blindfold is just a little kink to them, not a way to prevent me watching them make out?

(4)

SLING

"Jacobey."

I was stuck in the last few minutes of my chemistry lab, where the instructor was handing back quizzes from the previous week.

"Fromme. Pincetti."

Each time he called a name, the student walked up to the front and grabbed their quiz from his hands. I already had mine in front of me. B plus...not bad. Bored, I started checking for text messages on my phone.

"Harris."

Instinctively, my head turned around. I knew Harris a little. Well, not knew him really, but I noticed him. A goodlooking dude who usually wore tight jeans. A nice package showing, too. Didn't know his first name.

As Harris collected his quiz, he turned around and looked right at me. My eyes darted from his round ass to his sweet bulge, and then suddenly up to his face. He paused for a second, and then gave me a mellow smile, which was kind of like a sexy sneer. He caught me looking, I guess. Shit. No guy's ever done that.

Adjusting my position in my desk, I tried to appear casual. But when he walked by me, he did it really slow and deliberate. Like he was taunting me, maybe? Or was he just giving me a longer look at his goods?

I don't blush ever, but if I did, I woulda been blushing right then. Gotta keep that shit under the radar, man.

A minute later all the tests were handed back, and the class was let out. I started to leave, but then I noticed Harris hanging out by the door at the back of the room. No one was with him. I hoped he wasn't waiting for me. But as I got closer, he called me by name: "Hey Travis. Travis, right?"

I stopped, and kind of mumbled something affirmative.

"Wait up just a sec. I gotta talk to the teacher."

What the fuck? Why was I waiting for him? I thought about telling him to fuck off, but instead I think I just looked totally bewildered for a minute. Then the room was empty, except for Harris and me, plus Jones, the teacher, who was actually a grad student TA and was now making his way over to us.

Jones stood in front of us, his bag of papers and stuff in his hand, ready to walk out. He was smiling a little, kind of like Harris had done when he saw me checking out his junk. Jones was a handsome guy, nerdy little glasses but a ripe bod. I could tell he worked out. He always wore the same dorky clothes that they must make you wear when you're a teacher at a college, but overall he was kinda fine. He was about thirty or so.

"This him?" Jones asked.

Harris nodded. "He's the one."

One what? "Uh…" I couldn't figure out what Jones was doing there talking to us. "Mr. Jones, you know me. I'm in your freakin' class."

"I know. I know," he repeated, calmly, still smiling. "But according to Mr. Harris here, it's possible I can get to know you…um, you know… better."

Was this guy for real? Totally I'd let him fuck me, but he's my teacher, man! And how did he know…?

"I hear forty dollars is your going rate," Jones continued. "Or at least that's what Harris here says he paid for the pleasure of fucking your ass last week-end."

Hu-u-uuh? Last week-end…my mind circled back. On Friday after classes I took three loads from three different guys, all freshmen, back at the dorm. Friday night was a frat party, no sex. Saturday I worked out in the morning, and then let two roommates fuck me (not brothers this time) in one of the other dorms across campus. Neither one was Harris, though. And on Saturday night I got eight loads from a bunch of other dudes, all regular customers, all one-at-a-time in my own bunk, since Freddie always works the late shift that night at his job. But then on Sunday, after getting loads from my first two tricks, I got that text…

"Oh shit. That was you," I said, the fog clearing in my head. "Umm, whoa. Uh, I don't know what to say."

"Don't even sweat it, man," Harris said, slapping my shoulder good-naturedly. "You were lots of fun. And since it's been Mr. Jones here giving my ass that treatment lately, I figured I'd pass along a good thing."

Late that previous Sunday morning, I was taking this really cute, built little freshman jock's load up my ass to join the hot batch of cum some other kid had shot there an hour before. Just as I felt the first few wet shots of this little hunk's baby sauce fly into me, I heard a buzz and saw a text come through on my phone:

u do slings?

The message was from Kelan, one of my regulars. After the jock finished squirting his nut in my butt and I got dressed again, I left his dorm room and texted Kelan back:

whats a sling

His reply was a laughing evil smiley face and a message to meet him at an address off campus. Whatever. I replied "OK" and headed for my car instead of going up to the dorm. I had homework to do, but now I was kinda curious, and besides, Kelan is a pretty fuckin' amazing fuck. He's a junior, pretty tall, with hair so blond it's almost white. That sounds freaky, I know, but on him it's totally hot. He's gotta be Swedish or some shit. Plus his body is perfect, he's always got a tan, and he swings a monster cock. I love sucking it.

He also has this amazing little bit of peach fuzz all over his butt. I love the feel of it when I'm gripping his cheeks, either taking him down my throat or pulling him into me deep when he's railing my ass, which has been twice per week. For a few hours after, I'm always thinking about that perfect peach fuzz. But I digress.

I get to the address, and there's a bunch of guys there. Kelan introduces them—Bailey, Damon, Kent, Kyle, Spencer—and then we go down into the basement. I guess Damon and Kyle rented the house together. I was already totally glad that I made the trip. All of these boys were smokin' hot, and they were showing some serious wood through the skimpy shorts they were all wearing. I totally wanted to take cock from all of them. I still didn't know what a sling was, but I had an idea, and I couldn't wait to try it out with these guys.

Sure enough, hanging from one of the basement rafters was this leather pad, connected at all four corners by springs and chains going up to the ceiling. Kelan wasn't wearing much, and he pulled off what little he had on to get in the sling and demonstrate for me. Once he did, it totally made sense. I threw instant wood as he got in the center of the sling and then lifted up his sweet legs and hooked them around the sides of the front chains. His ass was exposed just enough above the leather to allow penetration. In fact it looked like maybe something was seeping out of it...so, automatically I stepped over to him to take a closer look.

"Dude..." I said, kind of in a daze at this perfect body in front of me, spread eagle. "What's in your ass?"

He shrugged. "Damon's cum," he said, glancing over at his friend. Damon was definitely a hottie, kind of a tall surfer type with spiky black hair. He was also nude except for his shorts, as were the other guys, but as he flashed me a cute little smile he groped his junk a little through the cotton fabric, saying nothing.

"Get your cock out," Kelan said. "I'll show ya how it works. Then you'll get in here, and we'll take over."

I felt a little funny. First of all, I always got fucked by my tricks—no exceptions. I never wanted to stick my cock in a guy's ass, ever. But the way Kelan was asking me for it, totally casual like this, and the way he looked so fuckin' hot in the sling... Second of all, I was here to get paid, and Kelan knew it. Fucking some sweet jock's ass, no matter how smokin' sexy he was, just wasn't on my price list. I didn't know what to say.

"Don't worry, man," he said. "You'll get your money. These guys are cool, and we got more stopping by." I still hesitated a little, but my dick was raging to get out of my jeans, so I started to unbuckle. Meanwhile, I felt the cum of the two freshman who'd just used me trickling out of my own ass, and I clenched down to try and keep their loads inside. After picking up Kelan's text, I'd headed over in kinda a hurry, and so if they were going to pull a train on my ass, it didn't hurt to have some natural lube up inside me for starters.

"OK, man," I muttered, resigning myself to the experience. "Here goes."

I pulled my rock hard dick out of my jeans, prying it forward painfully to line it up with Kelan's boy pussy. First I felt the wet leaking cum from his ass on the tip of my dick, and then a second later it's like his whole ass just suddenly slurped my fat dick inside. His ass was warm and tight. It felt so fuckin' good, right away. Now I knew why my johns liked this so much. I hoped my jock ass felt as sweet as Kelan's did. It was fuckin' amazing. I filled him up, and he let out a moan. I could tell he totally loved my cock. Then I fucked him, rocking steadily, feeling the chains of the sling creak and groan a little as I slid my boner in and out.

All around me, the guys immediately started moaning a little, like they were waiting for this. I got the sense they felt strange and quiet at first having a new guy there (me) but that they fucked Kelan like this on some regular basis, so now that I was doing it, they felt it was OK to start showing their appreciation. All of them pulled their dicks out, including Damon, who was still rock hard and looked ready to shoot another load any minute. A couple of the guys stripped completely naked. And one of them, Spencer, this farm-lookin' dude with dark eyes and a toothy smile, even stepped up behind me after a few minutes and started rubbing his big hands over my chest and hips as I kept thrusting in and out of Kelan's hole in the sling. Fuckin' nice.

I was already close. I hadn't fucked a girl in a few weeks, so I already had the hair trigger thing going on. But Kelan's ass was so much better than fucking a girl, I realized I didn't have any of my usual self-control anyway, and I finally just gave in to it, slamming five or six final times into him as I got ready to unload.

"Yeah, fill me up," he said in a soft, deep voice while I did this. "Flood my hole man. Good fuckin' sperm."

It was hot, hearing this cute young stud beg for my load. I closed my eyes and pictured my dick firing off in him, spraying his ass. Then before I knew it that's what I was doing. And as I shot off, I realized I was moaning the whole time, both from Kelan's tight ass milking my shaft and from Spencer hugging me tight from behind and letting his rough, strong, young hands roam all over my muscular upper body.

Kelan took all I had to give, but as I backed off, my cock still slid out of his hole rock-hard. A good sign. Now I could cum again while they're gangbanging me, for sure. Maybe even a couple times. I love that shit.

"Good fuck, stud," Kelan said, jumping out of the sling and slapping my ass. He grabbed my cock and gave it a few quick tugs, and then he even kissed me lightly on my neck. "I needed that, man. Now you try it out." While he said this, I got a last quick glimpse of his hot round little ass, covered with all that fine blond fuzzy hair. I also noticed the insides of both his legs were shiny with all the sperm running out of his hole.

I got in the sling, and positioned myself exactly as Kelan had done. My perky ass was lifted off the leather a little bit, and Kelan got in front of me to grab my legs and pull me toward him, so my hole was right at the edge of the fabric. Then he pressed his fingers into me, and smiled when he noticed I was pre-lubed.

"Sweet," he said. "You got some loads in you already, like I did. Perfect. So who do you want to go first."

I looked around the basement room at the other five dudes. Jesus, what a selection. Bailey was beefy, with long bangs, the total dumb-looking wrestler dude that all the fairies dream of getting on top of them. Damon, like I said, was sexy, in a pretty normal-looking way but that spiky hair gave him an edge. Kent was kinda a shrimpy dude stature-wise, but he had a tight body and a cool Superman tat on his left pec. Kyle had sandy hair, a couple of tats also, totally worked out bod, deep tan, and a pouty, intense look. And hunky farmboy Spencer was probably younger than the others, but he also was by far the least shy.

"Him," I said, pointing to Spencer. I liked feeling his hands all over me while I was fucking Kelan. Besides, this boy was so hot to trot that I thought if I didn't pick him he was gonna just jump on my ass anyway. The kid gave a big smile, stepped up between my legs, and pushed his way into my cummy hole. Fuck, he had quite the log…long and thick, how I like 'em. I forgot to scope out that part of him, but I was feeling it now!

While Spencer fucked my ass, Bailey came around to the side of me, and started feeding me his cock, which was mighty fat as well, not to mention uncut. (Before I started hustling, I don't think I'd ever seen an uncut dick before, much less had one in my mouth or ass. But I was learning to like them pretty fast.)

Now was when I realized the real advantage to sling design. I could suck cock, get fucked, and probably do five other things all at the same time if I wanted, and not have to worry at all about supporting myself or maintaining my position. Even back at my dorm room, in my own bed, where I took probably half my weekly loads or so, it was always kind of a drag to stay on all fours, especially after several guys had fucked me that way, or for that matter to be changing positions all the time. The sling simplified things.

Bailey came in my mouth, and I sucked it all down. His uncut meat shot off some mighty tasty jism. Then Spencer unloaded up my ass, and when he was done, Bailey was right there, rock hard again already, and shoving his meat up into my gaping twat. Two thick cocks in a row made me groan out of total happiness.

Kent and Kyle stepped out of the shadows to feed me their cocks on both sides, and as I alternated back and forth between giving them each the slutty head they were paying for, all the while Bailey slammed the hell out of my ass, which was already full of three cum loads from other guys—I realized that this was probably my sluttiest scene yet. I'd been at it for about one month now, and I'd done the group thing several times, but this was about as totally submissive and available for pleasure as I'd ever made myself up to this point.

Bailey fired off a nice big second load in my ass, and Kent went next, whooping and hollering like a fuckin' cowboy the whole time. It woulda been pretty annoying except he looked hot so he pulled it off. The tat on his cute chest bounced a little with every jab he made in my jizz-filled boyhole, and I watched him out of the corner of my eye as I continued to orally service Kyle and use my free hand to gently jerk myself off.

I thought I'd get Kyle next, but he actually went last out of the five of them. Kelan wanted my ass after Kent shot his wad, and I fuckin' loved looking up at this blond stud fucking me knowing I'd just dropped a big wad in his sweet ass as well. After I got Kelan's load he passed me off to Damon—the stud whose fuck in Kelan's ass before my arrival had evidently gotten this whole party started. Finally, after Damon shot his big goopy load in my hole, Kyle pushed his meat through all the loads of jism that were spilling out of me, and started his fuck as well. He grabbed both chains and really railed my ass, rocking the sling so hard that I thought it might collapse on us, but I didn't care. His dick felt great, and taking his load felt even better.

"Right," Damon said once the five of them were done fucking me. I started to get up, but he told me to relax for now. He walked over to one corner of the basement, grabbed something from his shorts pocket, and then returned, laying two pieces of paper on my chest that turned out to be hundred dollar bills.

"So that's payment so far," he continued. He looked me in the eye, then took out another hundred and laid it on top of the others. "And that's your tip. For a job well done. Cool?"

Very cool! I didn't usually make any tips at all. "Fuck yeah, man. Thanks." But what did he mean, so far?

Then he laid out three more bills, for a total of six hundred dollars. Some of the bills were sticking to the cum and sweat on my chest. "So, that's what we'll pay for the thing we wanna do next. You interested?"

"Uh…" I was suddenly aware that I was in a pretty vulnerable position, and plus I didn't know if these guys knew my limits. You know, all the shit that Cameron made me put in my ad about what I did and didn't do.

"It's nothing bad," Kelan said. "We're gonna tie you to the chains, your wrists and ankles. Gag you. And turn down the lights." He paused. "And then, after that…some of our friends are coming over. And we wanna let them fuck you, too. We want your sweet ass to be right here where all of them can just take it."

Friends? Who? My mind raced. In the dark, I wouldn't be able to see them clearly. "Who? How many?"

Kelan smirked. I could tell he was turned on. Probably did this lots of times himself. "Does it matter?"

I thought about this. Not really, I guess. I like taking cock from most any guy, cum too, and I'm good at it.

"We've gotta be done by 4pm," Damon said. "So, we're really just paying for two more hours of your time."

That made sense. My ass was definitely up for the challenge. Most Sundays I got fucked non-stop anyway. But now I wasn't thinking about men or cocks. I was thinking about Damon and his hundred dollar bills.

"I'm in," I said finally. "But I need another two hundred for this. Kelan keeps the money safe until I go."

They agreed to my terms, and we were off. The bonds went on me— just neckties, actually, and my gag was the same. Some of the guys must have already been waiting upstairs, because as soon as the lights went down, I heard footsteps on the steps. Twenty seconds after that, I felt a cock going in my hole. That was the first of about ten or twelve additional guys who all fucked me over the course of the afternoon. As my eyes adjusted to the darkness, I could make out enough of them to see there were some goodlooking dudes there.

But mostly, I just obeyed, giving my ass freely, taking cock after cock, load after load, moaning through my gag as one by one these studs all fucked me and flooded my rear end. I kinda dug the total anonymity of it, and shit, it was a pretty easy way to get eight hundred fuckin' dollars. At 4pm, all of the guys were gone, but Kelan and Bailey stayed behind to fuck me one more time and put two final loads in my well-fucked hole. Normally I'd consider this pretty obnoxious, but they paid well, and I was kinda blissin' on it by then.

"You were in the basement," I said to Harris. What a hot fuckin' thought. All these weeks I watched this hot dude from afar, thinking about what a great ass and package he had inside his jeans, and now it turns out I'd had his cock and load up my hole and never knew it. I turned to Jones. "And now you. My fuckin' TA...?"

"Yeah," Jones said. "Get over it. Harris says you were pretty incredible. And I can't afford a lot of crazy shit on a teacher's wage, but I can definitely spare forty bucks to drop a load in your sweet ass anytime."

I smiled. "You're on. Just keep them B-pluses comin'…" He got this shocked look. "Fuck that. I'm kidding."

We went directly to Jones's apartment, which was this shithole a block from campus that was above a little hardware store. Jones laid out two twenties on the futon and started to get undressed. Harris did the same. I stuffed all four bills into the front pocket of my jeans and then unbuttoned my fly and pulled them off.

When Harris pulled his shirt off, I instinctively reached out to touch his chest. He had really nice pecs. I could always tell that, even through his clothes. He also had a beautiful spread of dark, soft chest hair. It covered his pecs and made a nice trail below. He seemed to like my hands on him, so I ran them up and down a little bit. I rubbed his pecs, then his shoulders, and then skimmed my fingertips all the way down his back to his plush, round ass. As soon as I touched the area around his crack, he let out this little moan.

"You like that?" I whispered.

"Fuck yes-s-ss…" he moaned back. Shit, he was a pussy boy bottom, like me. Can't even touch him there without setting him off…this ass I'd been drooling over probably took cocks and loads on a regular basis.

"He fuck this ass?" I asked Harris, nodding toward Jones.

"Ye-e-eaahh…" Harris moaned.

"Every chance I get," Jones said. "I couldn't do this fuckin' job if there wasn't some sweet underclass tail in it for me on a regular basis. Each semester I end up bagging about three or four regulars. But Harris here is a special case. He got my cock in him the very first day after class, and

54

he liked it so much he's always coming back here. I think I've shot more cum in him than I have in all my other students combined."

Now that Jones was undressed, I could really admire his build as well. He was stacked like a swimmer, a fact that he hid pretty well with his geeky teacher uniform. He took a step toward us, and I fell to my knees, ready to suck both their cocks. I started with Jones's, which was tasty but pretty average, and then unzipped Harris's jeans and pulled out his whopper, which was somewhere around nine inches. I gorged on their respective bones for a while, delivering the fuckin' sluttiest head I knew how, and then we got on the bed.

"Take his hole first," Jones said to Harris, referring to me. "I wanna feel this slut's tongue go up my ass."

"Oh, uh, no..." I protested. "Sorry, Mr. Jones. I shoulda said. I don't do that. I don't kiss, rim, or fuck."

But I was already on my back on the futon, and Harris was sticking his cock in my ass while he held both my legs firm, and before I could stop him Jones was lowering his hot, clean, hairy ass down onto my face.

"Yeah whatever," he said dismissively. "You're rimming me. Go."

Fuck. I was pissed about this, and plus, I had no idea what I was doing. I wagged my tongue around a little, not really digging the taste but not really minding it either. Then, significantly, Harris plunged the whole rest of his giant dick in me, and for several seconds I felt nothing but pleasure and was seeing stars. Jones could have made me do anything at that moment. Getting nine fat inches up my ass put me in an agreeable mood. So, with a burst of I don't even know what, I dug my tongue in his butt and started pushing it around.

"Oh yeah...fuck, oh fu-u-uuck-kk..." Jones groaned. "Ah fuck, holy hell...you were born for this, you slut..."

Hearing that actually made me want to keep doing it. I gotta say, I like doing something well. So I did it.

Jones just sat on my face like that for a while, and I kind of started blissing out. Previously, I had sucked cock many times while getting fucked, but this (I decided) was even better. Rimming was awesome. It was like eating pussy, only with a dude. An appreciative, sexy dude. Who was paying me for sex. Fuckin' hot!

Before long I was totally into it. Fuck that, I seriously craved it. There's something about licking a guy's asshole that was just so fuckin' nasty and smelly, it was just totally hot. And like I said, Jones had a seriously nice ass, not just the tight round globes of it but a really good pucker: soft, pinkish brown, with some nice soft brown hairs all around it. Up close, it almost even looked like a pussy. I drove my whole face up there, trying to dig my tongue as deep into him as I could. Hearing Jones moan just egged me on.

Shit! I fuckin' loved licking this dude's ass! I couldn't believe it. Minutes earlier, it was a line I had zero interest in crossing. Kind of like I initially was about getting ass-fucked, I suppose. Now here I was, getting my butt slammed by one dude nice and hard just how I like it, and I'm totally licking this other dude's ass with everything I've got. I'm, like, the king of rimming all of a sudden. And in the back of my mind, I start picturing Harris's hot, round amazing booty, and I get an instant hard-on thinking…fuck, Harris is next!

Right on cue, Harris blasted off up my hole, and the two guys started switching places. Jones quickly stuck his cock in my leaking ass, but Harris was taking his time coming up to my face. "Get over here," I finally growled. I was fuckin' ravenous. I wanted to suck all the cum off his cock, taste my sweet ass juices on his half-deflated pole, and then rim his amazing fuckin' ass with everything I had—the sweet, perfect bubble butt that I had been watching and wanting and totally lusting after now for several weeks.

By the time Harris finally sat on my face as Jones had done, I decided this was an inadequate position for as horny as I was feeling. I made Jones pull out of me so I could roll over onto all fours, and I took Jones doggy-style while Harris bent over the arm of the futon and pushed his ass right back into my face. This was total heaven. I used my spread palms to open his cheeks good and wide, and then pressed my whole face in there, groaning as I licked his beautiful crack and devoured his cute little hole.

As I rimmed Harris, I thought over and over about him taking Jones's cock and cum loads into his sweet ass. He had the perfect ass for cock, and knowing he was slutty like me made it taste even better. Then I remembered how Ike and a few other of my regulars really got off on rimming my ass when it was full of…

"Fuck him," I said suddenly to Jones, sitting up a little. He stopped his motions in and out of my ass. I guess he was a little surprised. "Fuck Harris. Please, Mr. Jones, just do it. Fuck his ass and cum in it. I wanna watch you fuck him and then when you get off in his ass, I wanna try licking out your sperm."

I knew I was being kinda pushy, which took some nerve since they were paying me and all. But I hoped they'd be turned on by the idea I had, and would just sort of go with the flow. I was discovering some cool shit today, and I wanted to learn as much as I could. I already knew I liked eating guys' loads, and now I seemed to like licking a dude's butt hole, so trying felching (as Cam had called it) seemed to make sense.

Jones got this kind of wild smile. He pulled his dick out of my ass and motioned me out of the way. Then he stuck it in Harris's hole, who was still bent over the futon arm. Harris howled at the sudden intrusion but within a few seconds I could tell that this was what he lived for, like me. He totally powerbottomed for our teacher, using the futon and the wall as leverage to push his own ass back on Jones's cock with every hard stroke. He clearly loved taking Jones's cock up his ass and he couldn't seem to get that hot load fast enough.

I stood up next to the futon then, stretching my legs and pulling on my engorged dick as I watched my hot TA dog-fuck my hot fellow student's ass. Harris was so totally into it that his groans turned into whimpers, almost like a girl's. He reached back with his perfect jock hands and pulled his own butt cheeks open wider so that Jones could get his dick even further up that ass on every stroke. They were like a blur after a while, Jones pounding Harris's ass rapid-fire and Harris just whining like a fuckin' slutty little bitch, craving more.

Soon Jones was spraying the load in Harris's hole, and pulling out carefully to keep the jizz inside. A little bit started trickling out though, and it looked so fuckin' good, Harris's picture perfect ass just overflowing with a dude's cum, that without thinking twice I swooped down there and caught it with my tongue. Before the shock had a chance to set in that I was eating a creampie out of Harris's ass, I felt Jones's still-hard dick make its way right back up my bent-over ass where it had been a few minutes before. I was still relaxed back there so I took his fuck just fine while continuing to eat his cum out of Harris's butt hole. I gripped Harris's cheeks with both hands to steady myself against Jones's rocking motions, and also so my tongue had deeper access to its goal. Harris and Jones both moaned like crazy, and so did I. It was so fuckin' great.

I licked and slurped that fresh cum load out of Harris's butt hole, and to hear him moan about it, he pretty much thought he'd died and gone to heaven. I felt the same. The cum tasted so good. It was like eating a load when a dude shoots off down my throat during a blowjob, only it's even better and nastier than that because I'm eating it out of a guy's freshly seeded ass. Delicious. I knew then I was hooked on rimming and felching. As I grunted and kept wagging my tongue up there, Jones's load flowed out of Harris's cute little butch boy hole, and streams of it ran down my cheeks on either side, all as Jones continued to rail my ass.

Jones didn't last long up my ass either. While he shot his sperm into me, I beat off a huge load on his futon, grunting and totally intoxicated with Harris's cummy ass wrapped around my face. Harris couldn't stand it either any more, and he spun around to face-fuck me until his load went all over my face and shoulders, as well as down my throat. I sucked down all his fresh sperm and then licked his knob 'til it was totally clean.

While Jones was going soft in my ass and I was cleaning Harris's cock, I did that porno thing where I looked up at Harris like a total submissive bitch, totally worshipping his spent tool with his jizz covering my face all over. I wasn't usually this much of a pussy during sex, or right after, but in this scene it just felt natural. Besides, I'd discovered a new side to myself, sucking that sperm load out of Harris's hole while getting my ass fucked by our teacher. Holy shit, I told myself. Now I had a new favorite thing in the world.

At Jones's suggestion, Harris and I got in a 69 on the futon and Jones watched us stick our tongues up each other's ass. I continued eating out the load Jones had shot in my classmate, and Harris did the same to me.

(5)

PARTY

And so it went. I continued doing well at classes, and going out with Freddie and my other friends to bars and parties on the week-ends, and I even did my time at the library, buried in the books like a good little student. But other than doing that stuff and hitting the gym, all of my free time was spent making money at my newfound business. I had a whole docket of regulars who definitely grooved on my sweet ass, and I did everything I could to keep it in nice shape for them. I also sucked a lot of cocks, and started picking up a little money doing that, as well. Even Freddie, my floormate, started waving me into his room for some head on a regular basis, and he always came through with the free weed to hold up his end of the bargain.

About a month later I was on my knees in a dorm room, getting fucked by this kid named Pete. He was decent looking with an okay cock, but he always took a really fuckin' long time to cum. Like, over a half hour sometimes. It's a little boring but I like the regular business, so I just go with it. I don't think he cares whether I'm into it or not, he just wants a hole to fuck. Maybe I should break out my homework one of these times and just do some of it while he's fucking away at me. Anyway, my cell phone rang, so I got it.

It was Cameron. "Dude, what's up."

"Takin' some dick," I said. "You?"

He laughed. "Right on. Must be really good, huh. Listen, I wanna talk to you about this party."

Party. Oh yeah, Cameron mentioned it like the week before. Some frat dudes were doing an event at the house where they needed a bunch of guys and girls to provide service. So far I always stayed away from scenes like that, first off because the drunk party boys usually have trouble paying up, and second because I hang with a lot of the frat types and it's kinda weird running into them at one of those things if I'm one of the fuckin' main attractions, ya know? So when Cameron starting going on about it I kinda tuned him out.

"Right," I said. Behind me, Pete was getting closer, so I started rocking my ass a bit and clenching my hole.

"It's good money," he said. "I did one last semester, and I walked off with over two thousand bucks."

Okay, now he had my attention. I moaned for Pete to breed me, but I was focused on Cameron's proposal.

"You might not make that much this time, but you might. A lot of the same guys at this house want me back, and they said they're bringing more guys this time. So I told them they had to pony up for another buttboy, and I told them about you. They sounded interested. They definitely prefer fucking a jock's ass."

"What is this scene, anyway?" I asked. "These dudes gay?" I actually didn't know a lot of fag frat brothers.

"Some of them are, like the dudes who are setting this up," Cameron said. "But most of the dick you'll be getting is straight boys. It's kind of a tradition, fucking whatever hole is there, keeping it a secret. They know about the fag brothers, and they're cool with it, so this is just kinda their way of being inclusive and shit. And pretty much, as long as you're a sweet fuck and all you do is take it in your mouth and up your ass, they don't really give a shit about who you are or anything else. They just wanna fuckin' get off."

"Huh." I pondered this. Pete shot off up my ass, flooding my hole with his teen cum. "When's it go down?"

"Saturday," Cameron said. Three days away. "If you're in, you'll probably have to ease off a little between now and then. Prep yourself and get ready. You'll wanna cum a bunch of times at the party, trust me, and it's a little painful if you can't do it. Plus, you're gonna be fucked non-stop for probably about 10-12 hours."

"Right on." I pulled up my jeans, touched Pete's money in my front pocket to make sure he'd paid me, and then gave him a friendly nod on my way out of the room. His load felt all squishy inside me. Mmm, fuckin' nice. "Yeah, I'm in," I said to Cam once I was in the hallway. "Let's just go over some of the financials."

Overall, the terms were pretty favorable. We each got five hundred up front, plus a cut of the door fees, which were fifty bucks a head. (How these college dudes get so much fuckin' money to throw around is beyond my comprehension. I'm just glad I found a way to help them part with some of it in my direction.) Not every guy was going to fuck us, of course—most of them would be fucking the girls who were there, and it's pretty well known that the girls at those parties are drunk total sluts who don't get paid shit. So, a big part of the take would go to Cameron and myself, after the booze and other expenses were settled up.

I took it light with my clients over the next few days, and held off cumming completely except for once, when I was taking Kelan's cock in the back of his jeep. He liked to do it there, usually parked in some dark lot on campus at night, and I gotta admit, I got off on it, too. Anyway his big ol' dick felt so fuckin' good slipping in and outa me that I creamed all over the seat of the jeep without even touching myself. When he saw this he stuck his face down there and licked up the cum from the vinyl upholstery, which I thought was twisted but pretty hot in a fuckin' depraved way, and then he even sucked the rest of it off my dick. Then he kept fucking me and shot a really big load up my ass. After he exploded, he leaned forward on me and we both just sort of sat there curled up in a ball in his jeep, panting. I liked the feeling of his chest on my back.

But beyond that one time, I didn't allow myself to cum at all. It was pretty hard to do, for two reasons. One was that I was fucking this one girl kind of steady, and she always needed more. I met her at a dorm party and she put out pretty easy, so I railed her that first night and then I'd been doing her almost every night since then. I know she heard I was a whore for guys' cocks but she didn't seem to care, even when I showed up at her room smelling of all the sperm that was leaking out of me and stinking up my breath. She just liked my rockin' body and my big ol' cock, I guess. Or maybe the slutty buttboy thing totally turned her on.

The other reason it was hard to hold off cumming was that on the day before the party, Ike the sexy jock freshman and one of his buddies, a redhead muscle boy I'd gotten with a few times earlier, both wanted to show up and tag-team me. With Ike there, I knew it would get intense. He would suck off the redhead as he fucked my ass, and then after they both came in me, Ike would felch it out. I knew this whole scene would give me raging wood and I had to concentrate to keep from blowing my wad. As it was, I tried to get it over with as quickly as possible, even though I clearly loved every second. I laid there on my bed with my knees covering my ears and my eyes clenched shut, trying to block out the sight and sounds of hot Ike flexing in and out of my hole while sucking off his buddy. I made it through, but afterwards I needed a cold shower.

On Saturday afternoon, Cam came by the dorm to pick me up. Freddie was on my bed, getting baked as usual. Cameron greeted him in a casual way, while I finished packing my bag as Cam had recommended.

"Don't forget some extra towels," he reminded me, a similar gym-style bag slung over his own shoulder.

"Got 'em," I said, tossing in some poppers and an unopened forty-ounce lube pump I'd picked up the night before at the sex emporium out on the highway where I got most of my supplies. Then I zipped up the bag, told Freddie to keep his cell on in case I needed him to bring me anything, and Cameron and I were off.

"So, you ready to get fucked?" Cameron asked, slapping my back good-naturedly as we left the dorm building for the half-mile trek across campus to frat row.

"Dude, I douched, like, twenty times," I admitted, with kinda a nervous smile. "I just figured I'm gonna get load after load. I've been one of the top dudes at these parties before, and I always wondered how the chick could take that much fucking. There were parties where we were still banging her at noon the next day."

He nodded. "Yeah, this could definitely go that late, too, I guess," he said. "But don't worry. There'll be at least one chick there besides us, and you and I can split up the loads between us."

Cam was walking about a half-step ahead of me across the quad, and instinctively I noticed yet again how sweet his ass looked in the jeans he was wearing. Hell, Cameron's ass looked nice in whatever he wore.

"So what's your record, " I asked him. He looked at me funny. "You know. How many loads. Up your ass."

He walked for a few moments in silence. I couldn't tell if he was embarrassed by the question, or if he just needed some time to recall. I watched the tight, hard cheeks of his ass move up and down as he walked.

Finally he shrugged. "I dunno, I gotta say, around…thirty, maybe. Maybe more."

"That one crazy week-end you told me about? That time in the cafeteria?"

"Nah, more recently than that. I probably got close to thirty that week-end, too, but this was more."

Now I was quiet. My eyes were fixed on his fine ass. I pictured it full of thirty loads of cum. Then I thought about all those loads dripping out. I hadn't shared with Cam yet my newfound fondness for rimming and felching. Truth was, I didn't get to do it much with my steady johns, except for Jones and Harris, who didn't look me up half as often as I wished they would. Absently I wondered if I might get the chance to stick my face up into Cam's tasty crack sometime between now and tomorrow morning, and lick out all the fresh jizz that our fratboy clients were planning to shoot up there. Maybe Cam would even do the same for me.

"Why?" he asked suddenly. I looked up and he was sort of sneering at me, kinda mean but playful. "That turn you on, ya big fag?" Oh great. He probably caught me checking out his ass. But I didn't really care.

"Fuck you, man. Just asking."

We got there a little early. The gay fratboys were super casual with us, and we sat around drinking some beers before it all got started. The kegs were still rolling in, and a few of the other frat brothers were going around setting up dropcloths on the tables and some of the other furniture, protecting against the inevitable mess that a bunch of drunk revelers always make at these things. A deejay booth was over in one corner.

"So, the fuck pile…where's it going down?" I asked. I'd been to parties at this house before, but I couldn't remember where the sex took place. Usually at these things it was a big area set up in the basement, or in a series of bedrooms upstairs. Once a bunch of guys and me fucked a girl in their attic, which was pretty hot.

Clyde, the cutest of the four gay dudes, reached over and tweaked my nipples a little under the T-shirt I was wearing. "There's this big meeting hall upstairs. We mostly use it for assemblies. Wanna go check it out?"

Cameron and I followed him and the other three through the kitchen to the back of the building and then up a flight of stairs. This was clearly a part of the building that was added later. The main part of the frat house looked like a regular big old house, but after it got converted to a frat I guess they added this other space.

The room was huge, almost like a church inside. I think it was actually bigger than the bumfuck country church I grew up going to in my small hometown. Part of the reason it made me think of it was the tall open ceiling with these huge wooden beams going across. The room was empty except for some folding chairs, which Danny (one of the other gay frat dudes) started clearing out of the way.

Cameron and I stood in the middle of the space, looking up and around. "Don't think I been up here before," Cameron said. I didn't recognize it either.

Clyde was heading for a door in the far corner, which turned out to be a storage closet. "Yeah, like I said, we mostly use it for assemblies and shit like that," he said. "And usually for fucking there's a good space in the basement. But this party's a lot bigger than our usual ones, so we've got it all up here for the occasion."

He emerged from the closet with a pile of folded leather and some chains, which I instantly recognized as a sling. Already my swollen dick was jumping in my pants. Fuck, I needed to drop my two-day load so bad. And from the way he was talking, the party was going to be huge. I checked my watch—six twenty-five. My hole was twitching a little. I really hoped to be taking dick sometime in the next hour or so at the most.

"Liam, man, go get the other sling from the basement," Clyde said. "Brodie, help Danny with them chairs."

Cam and I helped Clyde hang the sling from some hooks that were in the overhead beams. About the time we had the first sling in place, Liam showed up with the other one. As we assembled it, Danny and Brodie went back in the nearby storage rooms and started pulling out these twin-sized mattresses, one right after another, until they had seven or eight of them lined up on the floor of the assembly hall. Along one of the walls were three long benches, like you'd see in a locker room but with padding on top. I could immediately see how they'd be perfect for fucking. I helped Clyde pull the benches out to the middle of the large room.

Then we all took a step back, and I realized we had transformed the place into the ultimate fuck party pad. The sun was starting to go down outside, and far off downstairs we could hear the deejay music starting up.

"Arright, strip it down, fellas," Clyde told us. To his frat brothers, he said: "I wanna start fucking these guys early, so they're both primed and ready to go all night. That cool, dudes?" Cameron and I both nodded.

Cameron immediately pulled his T-shirt off, showing his broad pecs and his hot little pleasure trail. Then he kicked off the baggy jeans he was wearing, and when I saw the red jock he had on underneath, I wanted to pounce on him and fuck him myself. Christ he looked fine. The other guys obviously seemed to agree.

Not to be outdone, I stripped down myself. I wore a jock also, a plain white one. I like wearing a jock at gangbangs because it keeps my dick and balls tucked into one place out of the way, while still leaving full access to my hole for all the guys to take their pleasure. This was another little trick Cam had taught me.

"Nice..." Clyde said, licking his lips approvingly. "This is gonna be great. Guys are gonna want to fuck those sweet asses all night." Then he looked right at me. "Hey, do you get felched?"

I just nodded. I guess he didn't ask Cameron because he already knew that was within Cameron's limits.

"Cool," Clyde said. "There's this guy, Jeremy, who likes to do it. I'll let him know your hole is fair play."

We each got in a sling. I took my time getting adjusted in the best position. "Go on and fuck him, Brodie, if ya want," Clyde said, heading for the door. "I'll let 'em know downstairs that we're ready to get started."

Brodie was a sexy, dark little hunk, with a really slight build but some cute stubble on his face and dreamy brown eyes. He seemed a little shy at first but when he pulled open his button fly and his engorged cock sprang out, dripping precum, I could tell he'd been dying to fuck me since Cameron and I first showed up.

I hoisted my legs up on the chains that held the sling, and reached down to pull my ass cheeks wide open invitingly. I had prelubed back at the dorm room, and used a butt plug for a couple hours that afternoon, so I knew I was all set for what these studs had to give me. I even bent my middle fingertip and jammed it in and out of my hole a few times, to get Brodie hot and bothered, and to satisfy myself that I was ready to go.

"What a little fuckin' slut," he muttered. "Can't believe a fuckin' hot dude like you wants to get it so bad."

"Yep," I assured him, with a slight moan. My own finger felt good; I couldn't wait for his cock. "So do it."

He lined up his fine cock with my ass and drove right in, balls to the walls, in one stroke. It felt like he was splitting me open, but I was used to that by now. No matter how much sex I got, the first cock of the day was always kinda a shock. I told Cameron this once, and he agreed, and said that's the way it should be—at least I know I'm keeping my hole nice and tight, which feels a lot better and is good for business overall.

As Brodie stuck his pole in and out of me, slowly rocking the sling back and forth and putting a wide smile across my lips, Danny and Liam talked about which one should fuck Cameron first. "Let me start out with him," Cameron said, pointing to Liam. "Dude, I remember that cock from last time. Fucker's huge. I need a really fuckin' big one right now to get me started. After takin' that plus a load, I'll be ready for anything."

So Liam fucked Cameron, while Danny (another totally hot-looking guy, and still fully dressed) stood to one side and started playing with Cam's nipples. Nice. Cam had these sweet, big nips a little bigger than quarters. After a bit of this, with Cam huffing and puffing at the slow deep-cocking he was getting from Liam's massive pole, Danny bent over and starting slowly tonguing Cameron's nipples. I watched all this, transfixed. It looked like total pleasure to me. And Cameron was definitely enjoying it. How could he not?

Then Danny's tongue left Cameron's nipples started moving around his whole chest. Fuck, the full treatment. I always loved it when girls did that shit. So far I'd never really gotten that much attention from a dude. He kissed and licked around Cam's sweet pecs, the V of his sternum, and finally up and around Cam's neck. This made Cam go from heavy panting to moaning, long and steady and loud. I could sense what was going to happen next, and I couldn't quite believe it, but it seemed inevitable: Danny's lips reached Cam's lips, and after a few seconds of hesitation, they kissed. And not just a quick, simple, let's-try-this-shit-dude kiss, but a long, sloppy wet make-out session. The kind most guys are dying for, including (I admit it) me.

Meanwhile Brodie, the short but handsome hairy-chested Irish-Italian, whose T-shirt was pulled up over his neck, was pumping in and out of me nice and hard, loving my greedy ass, loving the way I expertly clenched my moist hole around his uncut dick on every stroke. He called me a "fuckin' whore" under his breath a few times, and I didn't respond, but I kinda liked it. Guys seem to do that a lot when they fuck me.

Still I couldn't take my eyes off the scene in the other sling. I'd done a lot of fun, whack shit in the few months since I started whoring out, but this was my first time watching a dude get fucked at the same time as me. The combination of sensations was amazing. Physically, there was a nice big cock up my ass, filling me up and fucking me really hard. Emotionally, I felt like a total cum dump, a whore letting guys plow his ass for money. Visually, I had an eyeful of my total stud friend getting the same treatment from another guy who we both barely knew. The whole thing put me into this slut zone where I just never wanted it to end.

Fortunately, then, it was just getting started. Brodie fucked me until he came, and when he did, his slightly hairy hands grabbed onto my firm thighs and he grunted while he shot his nut into my ass. Then Danny quickly stepped over, his fly already open, and plunged his own cock into me, pumping me with about a dozen strokes. He had been beating himself off with one hand while he made out with Cameron so he didn't last very long. His load blasted into me also, and when he withdrew, I could feel it oozing out.

Around this time, Clyde came back in the room, followed by a few guys he'd rounded up from downstairs. I also realized that there had been others making preparations in the large meeting hall when we first arrived, who had been busy in other corners while we set up the slings but who were now curious what was going on and were standing around to see what happened next. All were frat dudes, of various shapes and sizes and degrees of hotness. To me, they all had the same thing in common: they were all helping set up a sex party, and they all had cocks that were ready to pound my ass and give me their loads of hot, fresh cum.

Clyde approached me, stepping between my wide splayed legs. "Yo' Travis," he chuckled. "Rock star."

I looked in his eyes. He was seriously cute, kinda a boy-next-door type. I licked my lips, staying silent.

"You gettin' what you came for?" he asked, reaching down and rubbing his crotch lightly through his jeans.

"Yeah…" I panted softly. Hard to believe, after just two fucks, I was totally under the spell of these guys. I know it was watching Cameron's action that got me into it so deep right away. I stole an extra glance over.

"Your buddy Cam's really takin' it, over there, ain't he…" Clyde said, following my gaze and looking on appreciatively. One of the random guys who'd been helping set up now had his pants open and was feeding his nice fat cock into Cam's face. Cameron sucked him eagerly, straining his neck to give him head while continuing to take the brutal fucking from sexy Liam. "Is that what you want, too? That how you like it?"

"Fuck yes…" I hissed. "Do it. Gimme some cock. I fuckin' need it. Uhh-hh…" I just moaned with pleasure.

"Yeah…you really like cock, don'tcha," he said, softly. At that moment, truer words could not be spoken.

"Fuck. Oh please, just give it to me…I want dick. Both ends. Fuck my pussy, fuck my mouth. I want it."

Clyde signaled for one of his friends to approach me on the side of the sling, and as soon as he unzipped I devoured his cock, taking Cameron's lead. He was delicious. I had been craving the taste of cock all day, without even realizing it. Still, my hole was twitching for more action, too, so I was relieved a few seconds later when I felt Clyde's shaft press against my wet pucker and then push right in. I loved it, and I was now dying to make him happy. I was glad I had a few loads in me already, making it a nice and creamy hole for Clyde to stick his cock into. I could tell from his moans that he liked my ass, which totally made me feel grateful as well. As I kept on giving sloppy head to the other dude, I started kinda purring, feeling content.

So Clyde slammed my hole and came in me, at the same time Liam was finally losing control in Cameron. The dude fucking Cameron's mouth switched to his ass, scooping up the leaking sperm with his big round cock head and using it as lube to stick himself back inside. Likewise, the dude I was blowing decided to take his turn, obviously sensing Clyde's true appreciation for my ass and wanting to feel it for himself.

I took several more loads over the next half hour, and tried to keep the parade of cocks steady at my mouth hole as well. I'd never felt more slutty, and it was fuckin' great. But after that initial round of seven or eight guys, things slowed down again. Everyone had cum in me or Cameron who wanted to, and some of them had to help out with final party preparations elsewhere in the building. Clyde and his friends stayed, but said they wanted to hold off cumming too many more times until the whole evening truly got underway.

So Cameron and I got out of the slings and walked around some, stretching our legs. There was a window where we could climb out on a roof section, grabbing smokes, and we had decent privacy so no one in the neighborhood could gawk at a couple of hot young dudes in their jockstraps, their asses oozing fresh cum.

Cam lit up his cigarette, which he'd found by digging through the pocket of his jeans that he'd tossed to one side of the big room right before the fucking got started. "You good so far, man?" he asked me.

He offered his smoke to me, and I took a deep drag on it, quiet for a second. Thinking, then exhaling, I made up my mind to be totally honest. "Yeah man, I fuckin' love it," I told him. "This is the fuckin' best."

Cam smiled. "Well, we ain't even got started yet. These guys are the fuckin' appetizer, dude. They're the nice ones. We start gettin' the other houses here, and the liquor flowing…fuck knows, it can be intense."

I took a second drag, then blew out a column of smoke into the early evening air. "The nice ones?"

"I'm just saying. You know how these things can go. When guys wanna fuck, they fuck. We're the pussies at this gig, and our job is to fuckin' take it. We've got a long night ahead of us. We gotta try and keep up."

I didn't follow exactly what he was saying, but I wasn't too worried. It all sounded pretty fuckin' hot to me.

Handing the smoke back to Cameron, I let my eyes fall to the wet spot between his thick hairy legs, where the fresh cum from his ass was spilling out a little on the asphalt shingles where we sat. "God, we're a couple of depraved fuckin' sluts, man, aren't we?" I said, licking my lips and feeling my dick jump a little.

Cam looked surprised for a second, and then he laughed and gave me a high five. "Fuckin' right we are!"

He took a few last puffs and tossed the butt off the roof. I followed his sweet naked ass back in the window.

(6)

PUNKS

Less than ten minutes later, I was getting fucked again. These two geeky freshmen both wanted to bone Cameron, but once the first guy was up Cameron's ass, his buddy was so close to cumming that he had me bend over so he could fuck me full of his slimy teen wad. I was glad to take the load, of course, but I was also a little disappointed, only because the first girl slut at the party had just showed up, and she was pretty hot: red hair, long legs, great rack. I thought maybe I'd get to fuck her before things picked up, but after my freshman shot in my ass I looked over and the redhead already had a crowd started around her in the sling.

Cam and I were over on the mattresses now, in the opposite corner from where we'd been in the slings before. The mattresses were pretty ratty but I was fine with it. I had a slight preference overall for taking cock on all fours, especially if it's a gang bang situation, and the cushion underneath obviously made this position a lot more comfortable. Cameron seemed to agree, as he was taking his loads doggy-style as well. I kept the lube pump I'd bought next to me on the floor, and even though it was about one-quarter empty by now, I don't think most of the guys needed it. I had plenty of fresh cum in me to ease the way. Still, when I had a free moment, I'd reach over and pump some lube in my hand, and then run my hand down around the lips of my ass, pushing lube and cum up into my hole to hopefully prevent being too sore when it was over.

So the freshman did me like that, doggy-style, and after I took his load I stayed that way, my butt up, facing away from the door, just relaxing on all fours and feeling the kid's cum steep into my jockstrapped ass. The lights were turned down kinda low, so the mood was mellow, which I liked. I watched the other kid fuck Cameron, which gave me a raging hard-on, but I was determined not to touch myself for at least a while. I wanted to shoot my big load later, maybe in the redhead's pussy, or maybe on myself while getting fucked.

Behind me, I heard a bunch more guys show up at the door to the room. They sounded kinda rowdy, and when I heard one of them whistle, I hoped it was in appreciation for seeing my ass up, ready and waiting. I was right, that was what they saw. The group of them approached me. I guess there were about five or six.

"Fuck, look at this sweet bitch ass…"

"Holy shit. Yeah. Fuck. Whole fuckin' lot better'n the skinny punks Clyde usually wrangles up in here."

A short pause as they assessed me further. "Dude, this is a seriously hot ass. I gotta fuck me some o' this."

I felt a guy kneel behind me, and heard him unzip his fly. He fumbled a little bit, probably a little drunk, but when he spanked his half-hard cock against my ass cheeks, it felt like a good-sized whopper. Mm, nice.

He leaned forward over my back, and I felt the fabric of his jacket against my naked lower back. In a low voice, he said: "So…does a horny little bitch like you need lube, or are you gonna take it just like this?" He slapped his hard cock against my butt cheeks again while he said this, nice and hard, which drove me wild.

"You don't need it, dude," I muttered back. "I gotta buncha loads in there right now. Should feel real good."

It took him another minute or so to get started, as he fingered my cummy hole with one hand and continued slapping his cock against my ass with the other. Then he finally quit teasing and slid it right into me, banging in and out of my ass pretty rough-like while his buddies groped their own jeans and occasionally egged him on. In between grunting and taking this dude's pounding fuck, I stole a quick glance around to see all their faces. I only caught a brief look, but they seemed pretty cute overall. The dude fucking me was a stocky stud with a little goatee. One of his buddies had his jeans open and was stroking off to the scene.

"Over here, man," I said to the jacker dude. "Don't waste it. Let me get on that dick. I wanna suck you off."

He came around to the front and knelt down so his long, skinny cock was right at my level. I pulled on it a few times, getting my bearings, and then inhaled most of it in one lunge. The dude really liked this. I think he liked getting a mean blowjob from a hot dude whose ass was getting royally fucked by his good friend.

"Oh shit...oh shit..." The dude in my ass was a real hair trigger, even drunk. "Fuck it, I...I'm gonna cum..."

"Dude, fuck it right inna 'im," the dude I was blowing said, suddenly all excited. "Fuck...that's so nasty, shootin' your wad in a dude's hole like this...go on, man, I bet he wants the fuckin' load right up his ass."

Hearing this, I took my mouth off his cock for a sec, panting "Yeah..." while I continued beating him off.

"Oh fuck, god...ye-e-eess-ss..." the big boy hollered as I felt his gooey dick syrup ooze up into my hot hole.

"U-uu-n-ngh..." I groaned as the fluid flowed into me. "I fuckin' feel it, man," I muttered, out of breath and totally turned on. "Your load is going right in me, right up my ass...I can feel your fuckin' cu-u-u-ummm..."

I went back to sucking the other dude while stocky guy pulled out and another buddy took his place. No idea what this dude looked like. Didn't care. I was devoted to sucking the cock in front of me, and taking it up the ass from whatever dudes came along. My slut trance was just getting started, and I hoped it would last through the night. As I felt the new cock sliding in and out of me, I knew I didn't care who was fucking me. I was here to do a job. I was gonna take all loads and every inch of dick I could get from all these guys.

The next two guys to fuck me had really small dicks, or at least that's what it felt like. I didn't care that much, as it made it even easier to concentrate on the first-rate head I was giving my friend with the long skinny cock. Besides, even though I was gradually becoming a little bit of a size queen in this business, on this night I knew I was in no position to judge any of the tops. They were there to fuck me, using whatever equipment they had. My duty was just to lie there and take it, and to collect all their sweet loads inside me.

I mostly tuned out the other action in the room, but they whole time this group fucked me, I was still vaguely aware of the other sex that was happening. The redhead in the sling was wailing like a banshee, taking schlong after schlong (from the sound of it) from god knows who. On the other side of me, Cameron was also grunting pretty loud. Other than the dorm brothers' video, I'd never actually seen Cameron getting fucked. Turns out he took dick up his ass a lot like I did, fast and easy, or at least that was my impression.

Before too long I'd taken the first round of cum loads from this group, including a goopy spray from my oral top who basted my whole face with his big sticky cum deposit and then fucked my face some more, getting me to suck him clean. I remained on all fours, relaxing and stretching a little bit, pushing my butt up, feeling the cum run into my hole, or else drip down the insides of my legs and on the mattress below.

The best thing I've found about the all-fours (doggy-style) position is that if you like really feeling a load go in you—like I do—then gravity totally works in your favor. A good top knows this, too, and if he's plunging in and out of your ass doggy-style, he'll crawl up your back a little ways just when he's ready to shoot, so his cock is fully vertical and he can just drop his creamy nut full-force straight down into your waiting ass.

As I caught my breath, I wondered what was coming next. The guys were conferring a little bit, and a few others had wandered by as well. Finally, the dude I had just sucked off said: "Right, bitch boy, we're all gonna take another round here. You wanna take it like this some more, or do you wanna get on your back?"

"Like this is fine," I said, adjusting my stance a little bit, but staying on my knees on the mattress. My muscles felt stretched, by whole body felt awake. I was totally game for this, squatting like a little dog-slut on a ratty mattress and giving up my screwable little boy-butt to all takers, taking load after load up my ass and down my throat, letting these frat dudes breed my jock hole over and over for as long as they wanted.

The first guy to get back in there fucking me turned out to be the guy I'd just sucked off, whose cum was still plastered all over my face and on the roof of my mouth. He got his skinny dick hard again right away, and managed to plunge it in me really good and deep. I was grunting for a few minutes, until one of the other guys (this really cute skater type) came around and plugged my face with his blunt little hardon. At first I didn't recognize him and I thought he might have been one of the new guys who'd just showed up, but as soon as I set into sucking his cock I tasted cum and lube on there, so I knew he'd just been up my ass.

Skinny cock fired off another big load, up my ass this time, and skater boy quickly shuffled around me to take his place. He got about dozen strokes into it before gruffly announcing: "Fuck, shit, I'm gonna cum…"

I actually love it when a dude is just about to cum and he says, "I'm gonna cum," or better yet, "I'm gonna cum in your ass." I mean, it's already obvious that's what he's doing, I just think it's hot when he says so. It's like he's so focused on how fuckin' great my ass feels that he just sorta panics and he's gotta say something, so he starts talking some bullshit about his wad. "Shootin' my cum in you, man…" Oh man, I love it. If I'm all horned up, I usually talk shit back to him, too, like: "Yeah, gimme that load dude…fuckin' fill me up."

After Skater got off in me this totally sexy new guy went next. I knew he hadn't fucked me yet because I saw him walk over from the direction I was facing, and he had all of his clothes still on. He was pretty tall, with a dimpled chin, kinda wavy brown hair, broad shoulders but a nice slim build overall. He looked like a jeans model. Total college boy perfection. "OK, let me go next," he said, and the crowd parted to let him in.

I heard him unzip behind me, and one second later I was getting my ass filled up with a hard, thick bone. Fuck, what a nice hang. His hands grabbed my ass on both sides, just below the waist, and he started in with a bunch of slow, firm mechanical thrusts in and out of me. This dude knew his shit. I fuckin' loved it.

Then he started talking some smack, too, in a real low, soft voice. "You want this dick. Don'tcha. You're a fuckin' slut." My head craned around. His beautiful blue eyes squinted and shone in the big, dark room.

"Ye-e-ea-ah…" I sighed back to him. My response was immediate, involuntary. I was under his spell.

"Mmm-mmm, sweet ass. Sexy fuckin' whore." Then, more thrusting. Same strong grip. I just moaned.

He was a sexy guy, whoever he was. I coulda stayed like that all night just to make him happy. I wanted to please him. I wanted his cum. I really wanted to feel his slimy load go into my sweet hole, good and deep.

"Fuckin' whore," he said, over and over. I went deeper into my trance. He was right. I was a total whore.

"Jesus," I moaned. "Fuck. Big fuckin' cock. Fuck me…" If I didn't take his load soon I was going to go nuts.

He rammed me that way, good and steady, until it finally got a slight bit more intense, and he said he was ready to shoot. "Un-nh…dump this load right in that hole, slut boy…get ready for it…gonna fuckin' cum…"

I was totally excited. "Do it," I panted. "I fuckin' need that load, man…I want it so fuckin' bad. Ye-a-ahh… Do it, just shoot it into me. Breed my ass, dude. Wanna feel all your hot fuckin' sperm. Fuckin' hot load. Oh fuck man, I need it so goddamn bad…just spray all that good cum in there, man, right in my fuckin' guts…"

True to form, he moved up my back a little bit and plunged his fat dick straight down a final time, keeping it there while he dumped all his beautiful babies straight down into me, filling up my ass until his load and all the other loads just went spilling out, sticking to my hairy cheeks. Total heaven. I couldn't stop moaning and begging for more and more of his cum. I started to cum a little, into the cup of my jockstrap, but then I held back 'cos I knew it would get even better. Eager for more, I stretched like a cat, pushing my ass up even higher, milking all that hot jock sauce out of his juicy dick, loving the feel of him pouring his sweet load right down into my guts. His load felt huge and goopy. It took over a minute for my ass to get it all.

After that, he pulled out, and I collapsed forward in a heap, my ass still in the air but my head lowered so my neck and arms could rest. What an awesome fuck. I couldn't believe how good his cock felt, and his cum.

"Thank you," I panted softly. I couldn't help saying it. I don't know if he heard me but I hoped he did.

While I rested in that position, I tried to recover as quickly as possible. I knew it would be only a matter of seconds before the next cock got shoved up my ass, and I wanted to be ready. I took deep breaths. My mind was racing with the image of this beautiful stud having his way with me, but I did what I could to calm myself down. I focused on relaxing my body, and especially my ass. It was twitching and spasming, almost like it didn't want that superior fucking to ever end. I struggled to get it under control and return to normal.

The next sensation, though, totally surprised me. What I felt wasn't another cock at my ass, but a tongue. Oh man, it was fuckin' great. Some pervy frat dude at this party was totally into felching my hole! It felt incredible. I stayed in my relaxed pose and just enjoyed it. Trust me, when you've been fucked rapidfire a dozen times or more in an hour or whatever I'd just done, a soft tongue is like pure ointment. And not only did it feel good at first, but it kept on going. Whoever this dude was, rimming my cummy slut hole, he started off soft and quiet, but then he really got going, and so did I. His licking got noisier, and he moaned a little bit while he did it. I pushed my ass back a bit, groaning with satisfaction, and the pace of his tongue quickened until he was slurping noisily and grunting a little himself. Then I remembered that Clyde had told Cameron and me about his friend Jeremy, who loved felching and wanted to offer his services to us.

Curious, I peeked around to see what Jeremy looked like. At first I couldn't quite see his face, because it was buried so deep in my crack back there. But he was fully clothed, wearing a striped shirt and a pair of jeans that was open at the fly, revealing a long, half-hard cock. His body looked fantastic in those clothes, and I noticed his cock was dripping pre-cum—or was that...cum? Hey, had this guy already fucked my ass?

Oh, holy shit! It was the superhot model dude who had just fucked me into oblivion. The damn smokin' hot jock fashion model stud who had railed my ass so perfectly was really Jeremy, Clyde's horny little felcher.

I grunted and shot my load into my jockstrap. I couldn't stop myself. I didn't even realize I was that close.

And Jeremy kept on rimming my hole, dipping down to catch some runaway cum in his mouth but then returning to my ass, plying it wide and deep with his thick, strong mouth muscle, soothing my well-fucked butt and scooping out one dollop after another of tasty sperm, starting with his own and then all the other fresh hot fraternity fuck sauce that was layered underneath, deep in the sleeve of my slutty cum chute.

"Dude...whoa..." I moaned, over and over. "Fuck...oh, dude...oh, man...ye-e-eaa-ahh..." I couldn't fuckin' believe how fuckin' good this felt. I just wanted this total stud to lick the cum outta my ass all night long.

When Jeremy's tongue finally left my hole, I immediately got filled with another cock. I was still blissing from the expert felch job, so I didn't really pay attention to whoever was now fucking my ass. I just relaxed and took it, and when he came in me, he got replaced by another dude. I didn't notice him much either.

As that second guy started loading me with cum, however, I finally realized my knees were sore, and my muscles were getting a little cramped. I'd been on my knees for the last dozen loads or so, and it was time to make a change. The bench looked pretty inviting. So as soon as the dude got off in me and pulled out, I stood up and told the guys I needed a break for a minute, and then they could start doing me on the bench. There was a small crowd of dudes gathered around me, all with their flies open, and they were jacking some mighty nice dicks. I licked my lips and smiled, then walked around for a minute to stretch my legs.

The redhead girl was still in the sling. I watched her moaning and taking dick for a while, and even tried to angle in to see if I might get a quick shot at her pussy, but the line of guys waiting to fuck her was crowded together pretty tight. What I noticed, though, was that she was quieter than I thought. The whole time I was getting fucked, and while Jeremy was rimming me, I thought I heard her squealing and wailing over here. In fact, I still heard it now. Had another girl slut shown up at the party that I didn't know about?

I followed the loud, crazy fuck screams to the other corner of the room, and even then I finally didn't piece the situation together until I was looking at it with my own eyes. The shrieking and wailing was coming from none other than my fuck-mentor, Cameron himself. Man, I couldn't believe how bad he was slutting out. He sure as fuck didn't sound like himself. He didn't even sound like a dude. He barely sounded human.

He was getting fucked really aggressively by this tall black dude, who I recognized from the college varsity basketball team. Dude had a big, long banana dick that he was plowing straight into Cam's hole, deep in with every thrust, all the way out with every pull. Fuckin' hot. But whereas if it was me taking that cock, I'd probably moan deep, loving each thrust—with Cam it was on a whole other level. Shit, he was practically screaming. At first I thought the guy was hurting him, but that wasn't it either. Cam whined like a stuck pig, rutting and wiggling around constantly on the mattress. He was on his back, his white muscular hairy legs wrapped firmly around this black stud's strong back, pulling him into his ass deeper with each stroke. So Cam wasn't in any pain—totally the opposite, he loved it and he just wanted to get fucked even harder.

I approached cautiously, not sure what to expect. When I saw Cameron's face close up, I saw his eyes were blurry with tears, and they seemed out of focus, almost crossed. His lips were parted, and he was sweating and panting and even drooling on himself and on the mattress. Then I heard the hot black dude muttering something low and steady under his breath, and it sounded like: "Cunt...cunt...cunt..." Whatever it was, his words and his forceful fucking and his fuckin' gigantic cock seemed to make Cameron totally delirious.

Then Cameron slowly moved his head to one side, and looked up at me. I didn't know what to say, but it wouldn't have registered with him anyway. He seemed to not even recognize me. He was pretty far gone. He was still wearing his red jockstrap. It looked stained in the front, like he'd cum already multiple times.

Seeing him so depraved like this got me totally hard. There was no way I could stand there next to a dude as hot as Cam, watching him get powerfucked into a quivering pile of jelly like this by some negro hunk, and not feel a total jolt of sexual admiration. Seeing my cock next to him, Cameron reached out weakly and grabbed it, giving it a few strokes, wanting instinctively to give it pleasure. It was our first time making any kind of contact like this. But I stepped back, a little freaked. Plus, I had to get back to my own slut duties. I also didn't want to cum again right away, which would've happened, and I wasn't gonna interrupt his flow.

So, with my raging hardon and my renewed inspiration to out-bottom my fellow man slut, I returned to the bench by the wall, scattered the guys away who'd been sitting there, and laid back on it to assume my new position. The hardness of the bench actually felt great on my back, which had been kinda sore all week anyway from a rough workout I had at the gym a few days before. I carried the lube pump with me and set it on the floor next to the bench, so I raised my legs up high, took a few big dollops, and then worked them into my boy pussy, pressing into the well-fucked, well-rimmed passage, which was already sticky from the cum of my last few customers. Then I just lay on the bench, my greased fuck hole open and ready for more.

I stayed like that, knees bent, getting settled, until this cute tan frat dude appeared, wearing a puka shell necklace and nothing else. Smiling, he lifted my feet off the tip of the bench and placed them on either side of his neck. He was a slim guy but he had good muscles across his collarbone, making a decent cushion for my ankles and putting him in position to slide his frat bone into my horny ass. Oh man, the fresh lube did fuckin' wonders for both of us. He slid in so easy and so good that we both kinda lost our breath for a second. Then he started in fucking me. I relaxed my arms down either side of the bench, and just let my legs and chest bounce up and down a little as this hot little stud railed my ass and gave me a nice hard fuck.

Things picked up again, and pretty soon I was turning my head to each side to suck other guy's cocks who knelt or crouched down next to the bench and got in range. It was slightly difficult giving head like that, but it sure tasted good, and I really wanted to finish them off with my ass anyway. Sure enough, the tan naked stud squirted his cum in me, and my two oral friends each took their place fucking my sweet hole, one at a time. Meanwhile, more guys came by and knelt next to me for head. And so, on and on it went for a while.

At one point, probably three or four loads later, I happened to look up and see a familiar face smiling down at me. It was Harris, my chem lab hottie friend who had tag-teamed me with his fuck-buddy Jones, our TA.

"Yo'," he greeted me. He was naked except for a blue jockstrap. "Looks like you be having some fun here."

I didn't respond, other than to reach up and grab a bare cheek of his delicious butt. "Mmm-mmm…" I said.

"Yeah? You miss this ass?" he said, teasingly. Then he fulfilled my silent wish and positioned himself with one leg on either side of me, facing away from the guy fucking me, and began lowering his muscular young butt down snug onto my face. I was glad when he took the initiative here, 'cos Jeremy's royal treatment had me in the mood for more rimming, and I wanted the other guys at the party to see this was something I was willing to do. Immediately my tongue snaked up into Harris' plush, bountiful ass, my tongue swabbing his spongy ass button, my nose and lips buried inside his round, hairy, totally desirable and fuckable cheeks.

"Fu-u-uck..." he moaned softly, as I eagerly licked his hole while continuing to take a solid, steady fucking from my current frat boi top. "Aw, fuck dude—oh yeah, man...feels nice...lick that fuckin' hole, lick it up..."

Then, suddenly, while licking and sniffing my way around Harris' hole, loving the musky flavor, I suddenly got a whiff of something else. Cum! No wonder his butt was so loose and tasty...some guy had fucked him recently, and now that guy's load was pulsing slowly out of his well-fucked hole. Hungrily, I ate the first few drops that spilled out onto my flickering tongue, but then I got curious whose cum it was, so I had to pull off for a second and ask him: "Dude, is this Jones' load in here? I'm tasting some really sweet sperm."

"Naw," Harris replied dismissively, in his husky, sexy drawl. "Some other dude. At the party, downstairs."

Fuckin' hot. This was a totally fresh load up Harris' ass that I was eating. I didn't know who shot it, and he obviously didn't know either. Humming like a dog with a bone, I continued my meal, tasting his cummy little chute as I pictured him getting his fine ass banged by some random frat dude downstairs at the party.

"Oh-hh..." he continued, panting now. "Dude, fuck—oh yeah, that's nice, man...oh, yeah. Eat that fuckin' cream-filled pussy...lick out all that good cum...ah fuck, mm-hmm...yeah, eat it boy, eat my fuckin' ass..."

The guy fucking me at that point thought it was pretty hot, too. "Fuck—" I heard him grunt, just as he shot his wad in my ass. When he pulled out, someone else replaced him, but I didn't see who it was because Harris' ass was all over my face, and I didn't really care anyway. In fact, I continued licking Harris' deep cummy hole all the way through my next three fucks, until finally Harris lifted his ass off me, giving me a breather as he took his place between my legs and slid his hard cock up my cummy twat for his own fuck.

"Yee-haw!" he bellowed happily as he whaled in and out of me. Fuckin' wild boy. I loved it. I took it all.

After that I moved from the bench back down to a nearby mattress, but I stayed on my back. The overhead lights in the room were turned down low, but were just bright enough to make me a little disoriented, and I decided I liked that. Besides, on my back I actually got to see how hot some of these dudes were, and in many cases they were totally hot. I was surprised so many studs showed up for a mixed guy-girl gangbang like this one. In fact, overall, Cameron's ass and mine seemed to get a lot more action than the redhead girl.

Speaking of which, Cam's intensity never really let up. The tall black dude had finished fucking him ages ago, but Cameron was still under some witchy sex spell, taking all the cocks he could get like some kind of totally depraved sex maniac. Well, actually, that's exactly what he was—the situation confirmed it. I had no idea he was such a dedicated slut. He was like a wild beast. I only looked over at him a few times, but his crying and wailing was pretty loud and constant the whole time. At one point I heard a really loud grunt from him, and when I looked over, he was sitting on a big log cock that was shooting cum straight up his ass while three other guys were beating off their loads on his face. He ate all their jizz, loving the attention.

(7)

BACKSPLASH

An hour later or so, the party had pretty much reached full swing. I was still on my back on the mattress, in the middle of the floor with lots of guys around me, some of them paying attention to me, some of them doing their own thing elsewhere. It was a great cross between a regular frat party and a sex party. Most of the people I could see still had all or most of their clothes on, and in many cases they were just standing around, drinking beer or cocktails, listening to the music and talking and laughing. Meanwhile, in the slings and on the floor, the three of us (Cam, me, and the redheaded girl) were all getting sexually used in every way we could, and totally loving it. I was in a full-on fuck trance, ready and eager for more and more cock.

It was easy for me to relax, because I was kinda just doing the same thing over and over and over, getting fucked non-stop on my back by pretty much any dude who came along. It was like what I did every day anyway in dorm rooms all over campus—same variety of dudes, just on a bigger scale. There were some dweeby freshman types, there was some real frat studs, there was even this cute, mouthy little prick with a punk haircut and tons of tats who sat his little muscled ass on my face and made me lick it totally clean while his buddy had his way with my hole. Of course I fuckin' loved this, and when he finally lifted his butt off my tongue to go take his turn fucking me, I continued to grunt and whimper and flick my tongue in the air, until some other dude came by and gave me his butt to eat while the mouthy punk was fucking my ass.

It was a really good run of cocks overall. After the first seven or eight, my hole was pretty much mush, but I could still do a little bit of sphincter control to help each guy along, and of course I clenched when each guy got his nut so I could feel every deep stroke and every blast of good college boy cum that went into me.

At one point I played host to Than and Paulino, a couple of cool dudes from the rugby team who I knew casually from around campus. They were fans of my floormate Freddie's weed connections, so Freddie and me went out to shoot pool with them once in a while and then Freddie would sell them some pot and we'd all get baked. It was fun being with them, because lots of times they used their rugby star status to help Freddie and me hook up with some of the choicest women. They lived in a house with two other hot rugby players, and I liked going over there from time to time and just getting fucked senseless by all four studs.

Right now Than (his real name was Ethan I think, but everyone called him Than) had just wandered over, unzipped, and dropped his cock on my face, playfully. I licked it happily but kept my hands at my sides, preferring to let him do what he liked. Than was square-jawed and had a super nice build, your classic QB. Paulino, who was shorter with olive skin, a phenomenal smooth gym body and shaggy medium-long hair, stood next to my legs and fingered the gooey hole below my balls, where gallons of cum were oozing out of my ass. He liked doing this after he and Than fucked me, too, checking out the hot loads inside my butt.

"Which hole do you want, bro?" Than asked his buddy. I secretly wished Than would fuck me first. He had a powerful way of fucking me that basically loosened my joints and turned me into a quivering pile of jello.

Paulino looked down at me with a crooked smile and pushed his fingers in a little deeper. I just moaned. Paulino replied: "Hm, yeah, uh...well I'm using this end down here, dude...why don't you try up thataway."

So Than, with his jeans still on, swung his legs over and straddled my face, stuck his fat fuckin' dick between my lips, slid it down into my throat, and started giving me a nice face ride on his thick, throbbing jock meat. I felt the denim pull tight against my adam's apple as Than started swinging his hips forward and back really fast, fucking my mouth. I heard some fumbling of Paulino's pants, and a few seconds later he was driving his long, thick muscle rod right up in my creamy hole. I really dug getting spitroasted by these dudes. I even hoped their jock roommates were somewhere nearby at the party so I could give it up to them, too, just like I did when I stopped by Than and Paulino's house, which was once a week or so.

Paulino's got kinda a hair trigger, so instead of tightening my hole for him, I tried to relax and just let him plow my chute loose for a while, so he could get some pleasure in before dropping his wad. Besides, getting a whole mouthful of Than's cock driving slowly in and out of my throat was a lot of distraction. I had to focus on giving Than sweet head in this position, holding my neck up so he got soft tongue and no teeth, and concentrating hard so I didn't choke in the process. He'd had head, I knew, from hundreds of girls on campus, and probably a few dozen guys as well, so I wanted to focus and outshine all my competition.

"God, his ass is so fuckin' sloppy," Paulino said, snapping my jockstrap against the skin of my lower back.

"Fuck him good," Than said. Then without warning, he started cumming in my mouth and down my throat.

Than cums a lot, but he doesn't shoot far, so after the first couple of shots in the back of my mouth, I pulled off him a little bit and I basically just held my mouth open for him, letting his cock lay all that hot goo right onto my tongue. I knew he kinda liked it this way, seeing his cum all over his cocksucker's face and mouth.

This set Paulino off of course, and I felt him blast his load inside me, muttering and swearing while he shot.

I didn't know if Than was done with me, because he and Paulino hung out for a bit afterward, chatting and beating off. Than's cock stayed totally hard. I had his cum all over my face, and was drinking it down where I had licked it off my lips and his cock. Several other guys and a few girls were standing around looking at me. I could tell a few of the guys wanted to join in, but they were waiting to see if Than and Paulino were finished. So I was pretty glad when Than got in position between my splayed legs, took his meat, and plugged it back into my leaking ass again. I'd taken 10-12 loads over the last hour or so, plus Paulino's, so I was ready for a big stud like him to give me a nice, rough fucking—his favorite kind.

I stayed on my back but scooted up tighter and closer to his body. I wanted him to have his hands all over me while we fucked—on my chest, my thighs, my calves, my hips, my ass. He set off chugging into me hard right from the outset. He had pulled down his jeans a little farther since my headjob, so now the hard, tan, perfect globes of his jock ass were sticking out above the denim. Weakly, I reached down and clutched them in my hands, letting me hold on securely for his fuck, and also to pull his big cock deeper up my ass.

Than railed and railed into me. All I could do was hold on and whimper. I was starting to feel like Cam, totally lost in sexual submission while the hot black dude railed his ass a few hours before. Than's ass felt like two footballs in my hands as he did me. He looked down at me intensely, grunting with each stroke. His big hands firmly grabbed my ankles and held them out to each side. I just fuckin' held on for dear life.

I love submitting for hot jock dudes like Than and Paulino—especially Than. His superman good looks, his total confidence when he fucks, all that stuff kinda brings out my inner sissy a little. I felt like one of those slutty cheerleaders we all knew in fuckin' high school, getting banged hard by the studliest varsity jocks. Meanwhile, Than's big dick felt fuckin' incredible inside me, pounding in and out of my well-used hole. His hard, furry thighs inside mine made for some friction as he pressed into my whole frame, pushing my legs out slightly, holding my ass open wide to accept his fuck tool over and over and to take his sexual attack.

Finally his gaze started getting blurry, and I knew he was ready to blast off again, this time up my ass. I had to get that load. I fuckin' needed it so bad.

"Oh fuck," Than muttered. "You like it, bitch. Fuckin' slut. Take it. Gonna fill up your ass with my sperm."

That got me plenty excited, and I moved my hands down from his ass cheeks to mine, so I could hold my hole wide open and receive his hot jock cum. "Yeah man, do it, I fuckin' want it, man. Fill me up. I'm a fuckin' pussyboy. I need your load dude, way up deep. Do it, shoot in me. Gimme that hot cum-m-mm…"

Than was usually pretty quiet—except when he was fixin' to shoot his wad. "Yeah, spread that ass…get my dick way down deep in there… yeah, spread them fuckin' cheeks man…hold that ass open…c'mon, beg for it you little bitch, you want this load, hold it open…yeah, show me where you want this big fuckin' load…"

I was literally crying by the time he actually shot. "Yes…buddy, do it… gimme all that good sperm…oh fuck, I need it so bad, man, oh fuck… fuck me harder, god I want it, please…I want your cum up my ass so bad…"

Then I felt it. His second load was bigger than his first, the load I was still sucking off my own face while I continued to rant and rail against this total jock hunk's giant orgasm. Than's load was so forceful I felt it in my stomach. I let out a long moan as he pissed his hot cum right into me, washing my guts with his sperm.

Than's cum seemed to go on forever. The total stud had an endless supply, and it was shooting steadily out of his monster cock right into my hungry ass pussy, quenching my thirst for cum in my butt, soaking my insides. I just laid there and felt it flow right into me. Fuckin' heaven. I never, ever, ever wanted it to end.

I think that's been the number one greatest thing about my new "job" and my newfound love of getting buttfucked. When I first started doing it, what I liked most of all was just feeling cocks go in and out of me, how fuckin' totally wrong that was, how it made me a desperate submissive bitch who let dudes fuck him because he needed money for his girl. But that changed after the first few weeks, and what I liked even more was the sensation of a guy's load shooting off in me, creaming my insides, filling me up with sperm. I was like a girl who needed to get pregnant, getting fucked and filled every I chance I got, except in my case it was totally depraved because all I really wanted was cash and cum. I always knew I had a great ass, and much as I act like a cocky little stud, I now knew I needed other guys to want it and use it for themselves. Getting their cock inside me was shocking because it was a violation. Getting their baby sauce inside me, loads and loads of it at a time, several times each day, was demeaning because it made me into a total slut.

Taking loads from hot butch hunks like Than and Paulino just heightened my sluttiness, and reinforced my need to be used. I could get the bestlooking guys on campus to fuck me and shoot their cum in my hole.

Finally the wave sorta subsided, and I tried to regain my senses. There on one side of me, as I lay gasping for breath, I noticed these sexy tree trunk legs, hairy and muscular as all fuck. Dazedly following up, I passed a hairy crotch, a half-hard hose of a cock, and a long pleasure trail leading up to a perfectly-formed chest, slim but ripped. Then I looked in the dude's face. It was Jeremy again, the fuckin' sexy stud who liked slurping loads out of my ass and then gave me that incredible fuck after. I didn't know if I could take another intense screwing so fast, but his tongue on my ass sounded pretty fuckin' great right about now.

"Dude...ah, fuck..." I groaned up at him, dried cum still gluing the edges of my lips shut in a few places.

He smiled down at me. He was totally nude now, whereas before I only saw parts of his body through his sexy dress shirt and jeans. "I watched you take that fuck real good," he told me. "Nice. Pretty intense."

I felt Than pulling his log of a cock outa me, but my puppy eyes stayed fixed on Jeremy's pretty smile. "You wanna lick out some of them loads, man?" I asked. "Got a lotta hot jizz stored in me down there."

Jeremy nodded over toward the space between my legs, where I was vaguely aware that another dude was starting to crouch down. I felt the heat of the guy's skin on mine, and I figured I was getting fucked again.

But Jeremy said: "Love to, man, but I think this dude's beating me to it."

I looked down. He was right. Some young dude with all his clothes on was lining up his face with my hole, obviously eager to sample Than's load and all the others that were inside me. I didn't realize there would be another felcher hanging out, but the fact that he was staying dressed and just wanted to eat cum out of my ass kinda turned me on. The next second he started right in, and right away it felt so good I swear my eyes started to cross. He wasn't as hot as Jeremy, but he was a cute dude who must've just liked eating out a slutty bottom's ass pie. I didn't see his face totally at first, just felt his big tongue moving fast and sloppy in my hole, like a dog lapping water. Fuckin' nice. I relaxed and let the cum run out so he could get it all.

When the kid came up for air a minute later, I recognized him from my Philosophy 101 lecture class last semester, plus I saw him around plenty on the quad. He's geeky but real cute. I think he's a junior now. He licked some of my cum off the pouch of my jockstrap, then took a breath and went back to felching my ass.

Then I gradually tuned in another voice nearby, almost a whimper, but growing slowly familiar to me:

"Oh, fuck me, oh, that's such a good cock…fuck, oh yes, oh man… gimme that dick…gimme all that cum…"

Was that Cam? It still didn't sound like his voice, but I knew by now that's who it was. I couldn't believe how intensely he was into it. As I relaxed and focused on his cries, I went back and forth between thinking he was just "in character" and believing he was actually a total slut who craved cocks and cum to the point of being totally delirious. His animal sounds barely formed words. From where I was, I couldn't see his face, but he was in the sling nearby, and I saw his sexy legs just shaking wildly out to either side as some big strapping fratboy pounded mercilessly in and out of his hole, makin' him whine loud and beg for more.

My felcher was doing a mighty fine job. All around us, guys were waiting their turn with me, but the crowd seemed to be thinning out a bit compared to an hour or two before. I didn't know what time it was, but the sun had long since gone down outside the window, so I figured it was about 10pm now, or a little after. My ass felt great. The geeky kid's tongue action soothed my hole, and I was already twitching for my next fuck.

———————

Over the next few hours, it went on like this, just guy after guy after guy of dicks up my ass and nonstop breeding. My perky butt was overflowing with jism. I went from the mattress to the sling, then back to the bench, and then to another part of the room entirely. My ass, I now knew, could just take cocks and loads indefinitely, so I got as much as I could. I was in a constant state of feeling all that cum leak outa my hole.

There were a few lulls here and there, a few smoke breaks and I even got a chance to rail the redhead…she was pretty out of it, so it wasn't as good as I hoped, but I still managed to drop a load. Mostly while I fucked her I was looking over at Cam, who was on his knees sucking multiple cocks while a dude with a backwards ball cap banged Cameron's ass and sucked off Than, who was standing all statuesque nearby. It was such a hot and fucked-up picture that I lost my nut in the redhead in less than a minute, mixing it in her cooze along with all that other party cum—basically all the same DNA that was leaking out of my ass, too.

Around about hour four or five of the party, a little before midnight, I was back on the mattress with my legs up on some random dude's shoulders, getting fucked. This cute freshman jock was sitting his round little ass on my face and I was licking him like crazy while a couple of his buddies plowed some really good cum into my ass. The one fucking me had a nice fat cock and so I was totally getting into it, of course. The dude I was rimming helped hold my legs up—I was getting a little tired by then. The guy waiting his turn to fuck me just kept muttering nonstop how fuckin' hot my hole looked taking cock. I loved this shit.

"Do it! Just fuckin' do it!" I heard Cam command suddenly. I looked over, and some slim, sexy Indian kid with a huge fuckin' meat slab was sliding all the way into Cam's ass, in and out, as hard and as fast as he could. Cameron clearly loved that huge cock and seemed to be going out of his mind, like he was worried he would never get enough of it or some shit. His eyes were wild and he was so intensely into it that I almost couldn't recognize him. His voice was deep but shrill. "I want your cum in me, dude," he screamed. "Don't you fuckin' dare pull out. Holy fu-uc-k, your cock feels too fuckin' good. Unh-h, uh-hh… Fuckin' do it, I'm a fuckin' sperm pig, man, squirt that hot load into my fuckin' hole. I wanna feel you juice me up…"

Then the freshman sat down harder on my face and moaned, so I had to get back to rimming him. The cock in my ass unloaded a big wad into me, and when it pulled out, the next one took its place. Nice fat one, too.

Meanwhile, the crazy shouting from Cam continued nearby. My buddy had obviously turned into a total fuckin' nympho. I couldn't believe it. One of the hottest dudes from my floor last year, not to mention one of the most laid-back and easygoing, and now here he was at a fuckin' frat sex party, getting his ass fucked non-stop for hours and hours just like I was, snarling and writhing the whole fuckin' time like some kinda greedy little fuck pig. Right now he needed cock more than any girls I'd ever seen or even heard of, even the wasted slutty ones who are always putting out for us in the frat house bedrooms and the backs of cars.

And it wasn't just the cum in his ass that Cam was craving. Throughout the evening I'd seen him craning his neck every direction to suck as much cock as he could get his mouth on. At several points he was on his knees, leaning ahead just enough to take a nice pump in the rump, while beating off a cock in each hand and going back and forth between them, giving them wild head and then slurping down their cum. He was a total sperm addict, gobbling the joy juice that guys were shooting all over his face and his hair and neck, then sucking it off their cocks, and sometimes gagging on them while they fucked his face and emptied their balls again deep in his throat. And the whole time, taking cock after cock and load after load up his hot, tight, pretty jock ass, in the sling or on the floor or wherever he was getting the guys to fuck him.

Pretty soon the shouting died down, I suppose because someone had stuck their dick down Cam's throat and so he couldn't shout orders for the Indian kid to fuck him any more. Me, I was lost in the sensation of rimming out that bubble ass that was squatted on my face, and loving the work-up that my latest mystery top dude was giving me, plunging into me harder and harder, getting me ready to take his goo. When this one finally released his load in me, I moaned so loud in the ass I was eating that it was almost like shouting through a gag. Seriously, the cum going in my ass felt so good it was like I was having an orgasm myself.

I thought that was it for a while, but it turns out the hot dude I'd been rimming had another buddy waiting in the shadows. This guy approached me with his raging hardon, and I spread my legs wide again, reaching down there with both hands to pull my ass open to accept his fat cock. All the sperm his friends had just shot in me made for good lube, and we got rolling. Handsome dude, looked a little like Brad Pitt but with slightly longer, shaggier hair. He fucked me nice and slow, which felt kinda relaxing for a change.

Then it got quiet again. I guess the party had died down a bit, because I suddenly heard a bunch of new guys arrive. I couldn't see, with the dude's ass in my face, but it sounded like five or six thug types, based on the smack they were talking as they headed into the room. They pretended to be all shocked and grossed out, and made a big deal out of calling us all "pussies" and "white sluts" for throwing such a lewd party and giving up our holes...but at the same time they clearly liked what they saw, and weren't going anywhere.

The freshman sitting on my face stood up for a second (his legs were probably cramping) and then I could see the other guys who'd arrived. Sure enough, it was five black dudes, dressed for the streets and looking pretty cocky as they checked out the scene. I recognized one of them, Kinzie. He was this big fuckin' dude with massive arms and a broad chest. He sold me weed once or twice. He seemed like the pack's leader. It kinda freaked me out to see him here. I never sucked Kinzie's cock or nothin' but I thought about it.

The Indian dude, who I saw now was wicked fuckin' handsome— he looked like that Slumdog Millionaire kid, a little older—had just unloaded up in Cam and was stepping away. A couple of his friends had been spanking their meat around Cam's face but now they stepped back a little too, as the five thugs wandered closer to Cameron and started forming a circle around him, looking menacing, grabbing their crotches.

Cam looked pathetic, his humpy body sprawled face-down on the floor but his cute ass pushed straight up. His red jockstrap perfectly framed the main event: his nice bubble butt, the perfect globes, the sloppy hole.

I caught sight of the cute geeky kid who felched me earlier. He was still fully dressed and was furtively approaching Cam from behind, obviously hoping it would be okay for him to provide his usual clean-up services on Cam's ass. He looked over at Kinzie, who just nodded. No sooner had the kid knelt at Cam's hole when something happened I'd never seen before. Before the kid could even get his tongue in there, Cam's ass, so overloaded with cum, practically erupted with molten spent jizz. Cum shot backward, one long stream of it, a few feet, like the party bottom's hole had sprung a fuckin' leak or something. The cum hit the felching kid right in the cheek—which immediately turned the kid on, of course, and got him quickly leaning his whole face in between Cam's cheeks to recover as much of the cum as he could get.

Cam writhed and groaned. He obviously felt some relief as he unloaded the cum he'd taken all over this kid's face. His hole continued spewing out the nut of the dozens of dudes who'd fucked him, and each wave of the stuff that poured out of his ruptured ass either got sucked up by the felching kid's magic tongue, or else spilled out around the edges, covering the kid's cute face faster than he could lick it up. The clean-up boy was in heaven, eating all those spent juices, and when he finally stood up he seemed a little wobbly. Maybe eating all those loads at once gives you sorta a contact high, who knows. Anyway, his whole face and shirt were now covered in cum, and although he'd licked up as much out of Cam's ass as he could, I could still see cum glistening on Cam's perfect hairy globes.

The whole time I was watching this, the sexy Brad Pitt-looking dude continued to slowly push his dick in and out of my hole. It's pretty funny, I got so into watching Cam that I kinda forgot I was getting fucked. He pounded a load into my ass and was immediately replaced by some big jock dude, but even though I took his cock just fine and gave him a good fuck, I didn't pay much attention to him; I didn't even see who he was.

I was too busy watching whatever the fuck was starting to happen with Cam across the room.

Kinzie gestured to the felching kid, who immediately took a hike. The other guys who just arrived were more than ready now, and they circled Cam's upturned ass, closing in, ready to pounce. Finally two of the biggest ones lifted Cam by his legs and shoulders off the floor and dumped him ass-first in the sling.

"So…beauty boy here likes dick," one of them said, a shorter, muscular one, cleancut with a great ass.

They stood around him. Cameron was a sight to behold. Naked, with the body of an athlete, but lying back in the sling and totally covered in cum from head to toe. Two of the guys blocked my view of Cam's torso but I could see his face and legs. Kinzie stepped between Cam's legs and felt around the slut's leaking pussy a little bit, getting his fingers wet with the fresh cum that was still belching out of Cameron's hole every few seconds, and then bringing the fingers to his own lips for a taste. The wild-eyed look on Cameron's face was a mix of desire and fear. I felt it, too. Even the dude fucking me stopped for a second to watch.

All at once Kinzie had his pants open and was sliding his gigantic black meat stake into Cam's hole. The look on Cam's face changed slightly. He didn't wince or anything, even though Kinzie's cock was as long and hard as a white boy could ever want going in his mouth or up his ass. Instead, Cam just widened his mouth into a big O and kept his eyes totally focused on his new dark stud top. Soon Kinzie was ramming Cam's ass like a maniac, still fully clothed but grabbing the chains of the sling to propel himself harder and harder into his white pussy boy's male cunt. Kinzie started moaning and talking trash, then just yelled louder and louder until he finally erupted, sinking his fat black tool all the way to the balls and shooting his cum gun into Cam's dripping hot ass. Cam just kept staring at him and gasped, savoring the new load.

Then another of the black dudes took his place fucking Cameron, and my top (a baseball player I sort of recognized from playing frisbee on the quad) went back to fucking me. He didn't last long. Watching the hot interracial fucking on the sling nearby seemed to make us both pretty horny. While baseball boy was thrusting, I milked his cock with my ass. I felt him deliver his babies in me about thirty seconds after that.

Then I heard: "Get d'at sweet boy ass over here." It was the short black dude I'd noticed earlier, and he was looking at me. He had his dick out now too, and his shirt pulled off, so I could see his fuckin' fine chest. He pushed baseball boy out of the way and plugged his cock into my hole. Jesus holy fuckin' god. I don't know if black dick truly feels different from white meat—I'd only had a handful of black cocks up my ass at this point in my career—but there was something about this one that immediately turned me on. Cam musta inspired me because before I even knew it I was running my mouth with all the same kind bitch talk I'd heard from him.

"Do it, man, use my fuckin' ass," I told him. Holy Christ, this muscle dude's black dick felt awesome inside me. "Just use it, use my fuckin' tight jock ass. Fuck, I need your load. My fuckin' hole needs it. Just put your cream in there…fuck, yeah…do it now, man. Shoot your big hot fuckin' load in me. I need it bad…"

He was nowhere near cumming, of course, but I kept up with the slutty talk anyway, telling him I wanted his hot cum inside me. For some reason as soon as he started fucking me I couldn't think about anything but taking his load, feeling it spray way up deep inside me. The way he was grabbing my strong thighs and just jamming his cock in and out of me in hard thrusts made me think that, when he did shoot, it would have a lot of force behind it, and I would feel it splatter all over my insides, hitting the walls of my ass, making a deep cum puddle inside me that would seep into me, just like all the dozens of other loads I'd got that night.

I got so into it that I finally tuned out what was happening with Cameron over in the sling, and totally focused on this fuckin' amazing little ebony hunk who was railing in and out of my sexy white boy rear end. Just when I thought he was at maximum intensity, he turned it up, and I felt him pushing into whole new areas of my hole. It was so fuckin' amazing after all these hours of giving up my ass to still feel totally energized and mesmerized by a new hot fucker. Since I was on my back, I could study every inch of this perfect stud, his bulging biceps, his sexy face, his strong shoulders, his horny gaze. My eyes glazed over watching him make his furious repetitions, pistoning my hole with his fat chocolate meat. I felt drool on my chin and realized that my jaw had relaxed open in a total stupor. I was slobbering like some cock-hungry slutty bitch who's so busy getting the fucking he needs that he ceases to do normal things like swallow.

When this little black stud's cum moment did finally arrive, it was even better than I thought it would be.

"Take it, slut, you take d'at load...take all d'at good nigger slime..." he grunted. He was gasping for breath and pounding me even harder. "Take all d'em nigger babies in your sweet fuckin' little hot pussy hole..."

It was like music to my ears. I shut my eyes grinned like a total faggot, relaxing my body even further in anticipation of the hot juices that would soon be flowing into me. Seconds later I felt one long blast of this smokin' hot negro's load fire off deep into my hole, followed by another blast, then another, then another.

"Oh fuck, ye-e-ess-s..." I hissed. I couldn't believe how much cum he was pouring into me. "Jesus, that's it, man...oh fuck, man, that's what my fuckin' slut ass needed...Jesus...oh man, that feels so fuckin' good..."

He filled me to capacity instantly but kept on fucking, and I could picture all that good cum getting forced back out and squirting back on the hunk's legs with every additional slam he made into my rectum. (Ike, my regular jock client back at the dorms, calls this "backsplash" when he's fucking me with his thick weapon and it pushes the cum already in me out onto his legs and mine. He fuckin' loves making this happen. Ike always tells me to make sure I have a few loads in me, filling up my ass, before he pays his weekly visit.)

When he finally finished shooting, his pounding slowly tapered off, and he made a few last thrusts into my hole and then stopped and just left it in there, his shrinking truncheon buried in my cum pot like a fuckin' soaker hose. To my surprise, he then leaned over me and grabbed me gently, in a way that was actually kinda tender. He was short, so his forehead only came to about my chin, but he pushed his cock in deeper so he could bring his lips up to mine. He gave me a short, sweet kiss, then moved his lips to my cheek and whispered: "I'm Clayton. Your hole is so fuckin' sweet, baby. We're gonna have to do d'is again real soon."

"Fuck yeah," was my instinctive reaction. I could take this dude's hot bone all day every day, and all night.

Then Clayton whispered something else: "Some shit's gonna go down here. Just roll with it. You be OK."

As I wondered what he was talking about, I started to tune in the action once again over in Cam's sling…

Clayton continued to lie on top of me while we both caught our breath. I looked over at Cameron. The lights had suddenly gotten real dark. Cameron's moans had gone quiet, changing into something else…more like a muffled whimper, hard to hear. At first I thought maybe he had a big cock in his mouth, but there wasn't anyone at that end of him. He was half-off the sling now, and two of the black dudes were right behind him. He was struggling against them, I realized. A couple steps behind them stood Kinzie, with some kind of big bottle in his hand. Kinzie waited silently while his two thug friends overpowered Cam.

I figured out they were tying Cam's hands behind his back, and they'd already tied a gag in his mouth. He kept on struggling against them until the two guys walked away and Kinzie stepped forward. Cam stopped struggling then, on his knees, facing the dark black hunk. They were both steady for a minute, and then Cam freaked out again and started struggling against his bonds. Kinzie's fist came back and shot forward, catching Cam's jaw and spinning him sideways on the wood floor. Cam lost his balance and collapsed on his side, hog-tied and—from the looks of it—half-conscious.

I looked around. All the guys from the frat party were nowhere to be found right now. We were alone.

Then the same two guys walked over again and grabbed Cam's arms and legs, carrying him to a nearby bench and setting him face-down on it with his ass up in the air. Another guy handed them a weird silver funnel (fuck knows where that came from) and then one of them pulled Cam's muscular butt cheeks apart and stuck the funnel right into his ass. Then Kinzie, fully dressed again, came over and opened the bottle he was carrying. It was full of what looked like tequila. He poured it into the funnel, pausing to let the funnel drain a few times, then pouring more in, until the entire bottle was emptied into Cameron's ass.

Fuck. A tequila enema. If I didn't know Cam was a hard drinker I'd think that would send him to the ER for alcohol poisoning. As it was, it pretty much knocked him out cold. He collapsed weakly on the bench, and after tossing the bottle aside, Kinzie grabbed Cam's butt and pulled it up to an ever higher position.

Then Kinzie started undoing his jeans. "Ai-ight boiz..." he called to his buddies. "Let's get started." He removed Cam's gag, which got Cam gasping and blubbering for a moment, but after that he calmed down.

There was some commotion, and I couldn't see any more because a bunch of bodies got in the way of my view. Clayton, the hunk that fucked me, got up from my mattress and disappeared somewhere in the crowd.

That's when I suddenly realized that more guys were showing up, buddies of Kinzie I'm guessing. Dozens of dudes made their way into the room, lining up around Cam's bench position, unbuckling their pants and moving in. I couldn't see them all real clearly at first, but it was definitely a different mix of guys than we'd seen earlier in the party. They were a little older, like mid to late twenties, and they pretty much all seemed to be black, hispanic, or some combination of both. Most of them had stripped to the waist, a few were totally nude, and I could see that for gangbangers they were all in good shape. Hot thugs, basically. I caught sight of several who had their flies open and without exception they were all swingin' some serious meat... fuckin' huge in fact. Big throbbing uncut blatino cocks, beer can thick, dripping precum, ready for service.

The first one up had a giant monster dick, big enough I thought it was gonna rip Cam open, but it actually ended up sliding right in. Cam jerked slightly upward at the intrusion and gave a little grunt, but it sounded like a good grunt, and anyway, he was mostly unconscious at this point. The dude up his ass immediately grabbed Cam's cheeks tight on both sides and started hammering that huge thing in and out of him, rapid fire. Cam looked so lifeless that I thought he was out cold for sure by now—even his stretched cooze had to feel some pain from this kind of treatment if he was actually awake—but sure enough, a couple minutes in, I heard him moaning, even mumbling a little, that whole fuck-trance thing he goes into when he can't get enough cock. Hearing he was awake, a slim tall dude stepped up and stuck his meat into Cam's mouth. As fucked up as he was, Cam rose to the occasion and dutifully started applying some really good head.

I started getting hard as I watched my zonked-out buddy, slung face-first over a bench like a sack of potatoes, getting raped at both ends by fuckin' huge delicious-looking black cocks. The rest of the guys stood around beating off, waiting their turn, and although they weren't saying much, I could tell they were getting impatient. Their cocks stuck out through the fronts of their pants and shorts, hard as steel, ready to fuck. They fuckin' reminded me of wild animals surrounding a fresh kill. Every one of them wanted a taste.

What the fuck was happening? I'd really been digging this party up 'til now. I had kinda figured it would be wrapping up soon, which made me sad because my ass was getting so much good cock, but that was before these dudes showed up. They were hot, but I was scared. Whoever they were, they were serious about using Cam and me on a whole other level than all those other college types who'd fucked us the past several hours. Who by the way were nowhere to be seen all of a sudden, like I said. It all had the look of a setup.

Jesus Christ. Someone sold us out. Was it Clyde, the homo frat dude? Or one of his buddies? No way this party had just suddenly turned into a total thug gangbang. And now that it was, things were getting nasty. What would happen to Cam? What was gonna happen to me? Did anyone even remember I was here?

I looked over, and Clayton, the black dude who just fucked me, was walking my way again. It was like he could hear my thoughts. He looked at me, totally intense. Fuck, he's hot, I said to myself. I thought maybe he was going to explain, but when he got over to me just stuck his cock in my face and made me suck him for a while. I was pissed at first because I wanted to keep my eye on Cam and make sure he was OK. But Clayton's cock was so intoxicating, covered in his fresh cum and my ass slime, that I couldn't stop sucking it, and pretty soon the only thing in my thoughts was worshipping the beautiful hot black cock in my hands.

I was up off my mattress and on my knees at this point, so when I saw in my peripheral vision that a few of the guys who were watching us started moving around behind me, I instinctively pressed my sweet ass up in the air, letting them know I was fully available to be fucked and bred. Turns out I really didn't have to bother. These dudes were very much in the mood to just take what I had to offer, whether I gave it willingly or not. I felt rough hands on my ass, jerking me into position, followed by a hard slap against my cheeks. I had tricks before who were into a little light spanking, but this slap went beyond that. Dude slapped me fuckin' hard. So hard I choked on Clayton's dick and my impulse was to spin around and tell the dude he was being an asshole. But these guys weren't having any of that.

Clayton grabbed my head and started skull-fucking me good and hard, saying, "Fuckin' bitch, you'll fuckin' keep your mouth on my dick while these guys do what the fuck they want, and you'll fuckin' like it." All the tenderness from our post-fuck cuddle was obviously gone. He said it in a growl, and even though I tried to struggle against him, the truth was I was still choking badly on his big dick, so my first priority was getting this blowjob back under control. I never quite did that, but I did stop struggling, and at least a few seconds later I could breathe again. Meanwhile the guys behind me kept smacking my ass and the sides of my hips, calling me a whore, hitting me with their fists and open palms, over and over, harder and harder each time.

I didn't get it. I was giving my ass to them. I liked being fucked. Liked it a LOT. So why knock me around?

Clayton's skull fucking was giving me a head rush. I was powerless to do anything but just take it. I hoped he might cum quickly, but given the huge load he'd shot up my ass a few minutes earlier, that didn't seem real likely. Finally the constant blows to my ass stopped and I felt a long, skinny dick going into my hole. It was a relief to take it all. Getting my ass fucked, I decided, was a whole lot more comfortable than getting it smacked around. I milked the dude's bone with my hole, as I had been trained to do, but that just seemed to piss him off. "Just fuckin' lay there, slut," he told me, "or we fuck you up." So, naturally, I obeyed.

All in all three guys came up my ass while Clayton was fucking my face. I tried to focus on relaxing, as they were obviously only satisfied if my whole body was totally limp. It felt good to take their sperm in me, including Clayton's second load down my throat, but it also felt humiliating, not to mention fuckin' painful, to do all the stuff I was doing under threat of violence. Still, I realized, I pretty much had a raging hardon from the second these dudes all showed up. I couldn't figure out this scene. Did I like it, or not?

Before I could ponder that, Kinzie walked over carrying something. "You done?" he asked. He was asking my tops, of course (who must have all nodded) but for some reason I thought he was talking to me. Behind him, Cam was wailing like a banshee as Kinzie's minions did god knows what, but I wasn't really tuning that in any more. When I looked up at Kinzie to reply, he stuffed a white rag in my face. It smelled funny.

"Sniff," he said. That's the last thing I remember for a while.

(8)

BASEMENT

I woke up to the feeling of a big cock going in and out of my ass. Not that unusual, you'd think, but it took me a long time to get my bearings. The room was pitch dark, and my head was a drug-induced fog. At first, I didn't remember I was ever at a party. I didn't remember Cameron or the black dudes. I had some kind of wicked dream, but I didn't remember what it was. I didn't even remember that I liked taking dude's cocks up my ass, but I was taking one now. It was pretty unreal. Me, on my back, somehow swinging forward and backward through the air a little above the ground, while getting my asshole repeatedly violated by some random dude's big cock. I didn't quite remember I was a male whore, and I did this all the time. There were noises around me, and voices, but I didn't know whose they were. Gradually I figured out I was in a sling, and when I remembered what that was, the rest started coming back to me, too. But slowly.

The next thing I noticed was that my hands were up above me, cuffed to the chains on the sides of the sling. Panicked, I started waving my arms, but they didn't budge, and I quickly realized I was way too fatigued to put up any kind of struggle anyway. My whole body felt dense and heavy, like it was made out of wood. I could move my legs around, but the guy fucking me was standing in between them, so even though I was flailing to get free, I just ended up wrapping myself around his body, and pulling his dick deeper in my ass.

"He's up," said a voice on my left.

"Right," said my top. "Hold him still now. I wanna add my load in there. Wanna get it real deep in his ass."

A low light clicked on, and my eyes started to adjust. A couple of guys grabbed my arms and my spread-eagle legs, holding me in one place so the dude fucking me could finish. Fuck, he was a handsome dude. Big strong latino fucker, slicked back hair, stubbly goatee. I just watched him slack-jawed and felt his cock pile-drive into me in long, steady strides, until he let loose a big cum load that spilled out around his cock and dropped, sloppily and audibly, onto the floor. Something about the sound it made seemed odd. Like it was a concrete floor. But the frat house room had wood floors. Even in my half-conscious state I put it together: We were somewhere else now. The "party" had moved.

"Okay, that's sixteen total," said another dude standing nearby. "Not bad for bein' out of it the whole time. Now he's up we can spin him around some and get him sucking us too." Dude had a fuckin' clipboard and was making notes. I took this to mean my ass got bred with sixteen loads total while I was knocked out.

So more hands grabbed me roughly and started shifting me around. Now that I was awake, they seemed to have further plans for me. They left my hands cuffed but they unhooked the cuffs from the top of the sling, so they could maneuver me around a little better I guess. Somehow I ended up on my stomach, still in the sling, with my knees spread wide out to the spots where the chains attached, putting my ass straight up in the air where they wanted it. The lighting sucked and I was plenty dizzy, but I got a sort of peek around as they were manhandling me, and what I noticed was that the place was still full of guys. I couldn't tell if they were the same guys from earlier, but it seemed like it…big, naked, macho black and latino hunks, all just standing around, watching the scene, waiting for their turn to rape the hot little white college dude in the sling.

But you can't rape the willing, I suddenly heard a voice say in my head. Yeah, that was bullshit. Or was it? I had come to this party voluntarily, knowing I was giving up my ass and my body to any number of dudes. I did it for money, but who am I kidding, as soon as those first few dicks were inside me I knew it fuckin' turned me on to be the center of attention for a room full of horny guys. Hell, look at Cameron and how he totally bitched out for those cocks. I was starting to understand how much he liked it, and why he liked it so much. When you know you're a good piece of ass, something in you just wants to give it away, again and again. Something in me wants that, anyway. Forty dollars, or no forty dollars. When it came right down to it, I was now just a slut who needed cock, and needed it badly. So why not a whole gang of rough dudes in the middle of the night, using my holes and pushing me around to do whatever the hell else they wanted?

And by the way…where the fuck was Cameron in all of this? Last I saw him, Kinzie's boys were devouring and destroying his ass. He had been screaming with pain and pleasure. Now I didn't hear him any more…

The fucking resumed. I took big, dark dicks in my mouth and ass for well over an hour, never moving from my awkward position on my knees in the sling. I kept my back arched not to choke too badly. Finally I got a short break where the cocks in my mouth moved aside, and I could take a minute to swallow all the cum they'd given me. Immediately following that, I felt the rag on my face again, and I was out like a light.

When I came to again I was in a totally different position. My knees were on a cold concrete floor, and a cock was going into me at either end. So this time they didn't even wait for me to wake up before they started face-fucking me. I guess if I'm sleeping I'm relaxed and they can get their own head. The one up my ass had probably been fucking me for a while, but the one going down my throat made me gag a little and that's probably what woke me up. I remembered the scene a lot faster this time, and I didn't want to get knocked out again by the rag, so I stayed as limp and submissive as possible, almost like I was still asleep.

I liked the taste of the cock I was sucking, and it was a perfect size, so as I got a little less scared I started getting into sucking it more. I bobbed my head on it, like a good slut. The dude I was sucking appreciated this, giving a moan and a chuckle. "Oh, someone's awake," he said. From his voice he sounded like a black dude, probably a little older than me, but who knows. "You suck it good, boy, and we'll be nice to you."

I went on sucking, more vigorously. Jesus, this cock tasted sweet. I wanted to make it cum. Noticing my energy, the guy fucking me slapped my ass and picked up the pace a little.

"Oh ye-e-eahh, horny lil' cock-bitch…" my fucker said. "Fuck. I love it when they wake up and they know they can't do shit but just stay there. Take my fuckin' cock, you hot little beauty fuckin' white whore."

I felt turned on but also incredibly tired. It took every muscle in my body and every last bit of strength I had to keep up with the sex. I was skewered between two totally unknown guys, giving head to one and using the rocking motion of my hot little body to fuck myself up and down on the dude's bone who was crouched at my ass. Jesus, I really was a slut. It was one thing to take cock after cock at a frat party, or to let dudes pay me a few bills to shoot their cream in my asshole. But it was another thing to get knocked out and then have my sweet jock ass pimped out all night to a roomful—or was it a houseful?—of total strangers.

While these guys were working me over, I heard the creak of a doorway, and a sliver of light came in the room. I stayed focused on what I was doing, fearful that if I did the wrong thing I'd get the rag again.

"How's that slut doing?" came a voice, behind and above us. I figured out we were in some basement, and the open doorway was at the top of some stairs.

"Good, good..." answered my oral top, again with a light chuckle. "We'll be done down here in just a little bit. Party wrapping up yet with that other boy upstairs?"

"Not just yet. Soon." The voice on the stairs paused, and I used the available light to try sneaking a peek around me. In my position, though, I couldn't see much. "Well, just bring him on up when he's done."

The door shut again, and we were back in darkness. I sucked the dude's cock in front of me, savoring his musky crotch and delicious bone, until he suddenly started spewing in my mouth. His cum was tasty, but not as tasty as his cock. I hummed and groaned and made a lot of slutty noises as I gobbled down his load.

This got the guy behind me excited, and he let his own cum fly in my ass. Not that I could feel anything back there. I was pretty sure at this point that, while I was unconscious, I had been ass-raped repeatedly by several dozen guys. There was so much cum leaking out of me that my thighs felt like they were stuck together. My ass was numb, but it didn't hurt. I wondered if I'd gotten a special alcohol enema, as well.

Dude behind me pulled out, and I heard him walk across the room. He switched on a small lamp, and after a few seconds of blinking, I could see we were indeed in the basement of some shitty house. I spat out the other dude's cock, finished swallowing the last of his cum, and shakily leaned back onto my haunches. My eyes started to focus better, and the first thing I looked at was the happy, smiling face of the guy whose load I'd just taken in my mouth. He was, like, sixty fuckin' years old. The other guy was younger, thirties probably, skinny but goodlooking. Not really a thug, just an average guy, real cute. Both guys were black.

"I'm Otis," the older guy said politely. "This is my house. Lamont here, he's my son. He's a good boy."

Right. Uh, this was too twisted. Holy fuck…I was in some kinda fuckin' twilight zone shit. Cum poured outa my ass onto the cement floor but I didn't care, and it looked like they didn't either. I got a better look at Lamont, who was walking around, picking up a bunch of little towels that I guess other guys must have used to wipe off after they were done fucking me. Lamont was tall, really handsome, with a cover of even stubble on his face, close cropped hair, and a thin, fine muscular build. His dick swinging down, now soft, was still eight inches. He was definitely hot, but I couldn't believe I'd sucked off his senior citizen of a fuckin' father. Probably got fucked by him, too. Then again, I probably got fucked by every different type of guy that night…every size, every shape, every age, every color. Fuck. I was such a fuckin' slutty whore.

I didn't know what to say—nice to meet you, Otis?—so I just let him go on talking. With any luck I'd be outa there soon. I tried not to look at him, but I did sneak a peek back at that delicious cock. It was almost as big as Lamont's giant sausage. I licked my lips, thinking about how great it felt having it stuffed into my face.

"We like having boys like you over, special boys. And those boys on campus, they're so good about letting us in on some of the good things they have, like you. Such a nice boy. You let us use you really well."

"Yeah," Lamont said, his voice a low growl. "Real fuckin' sweet. You the best white bitches we ever had."

Bitches. I forgot about Cameron. Where was he? Was he alright? "Where am I? And where's my friend?"

Lamont ignored the first question, but in response to the other question, he just looked up at the basement ceiling rafters and stayed quiet for a minute. Above us, I could hear the faint sound of bedsprings bouncing up and down. "Still busy, I guess," he said. "Jesus, ya know, that fuckin' slut's even hornier than you are. We had every dude we could think of come by the house and just pile drive 'im, and he still can't fuckin' get enough. That white boy's ass was simply made for breeding." I immediately pictured Cam's ass, and I had to agree. Based on how hot it was and what I'd seen that night, his sweet ass was fuckin' insatiable. It made me wonder how Cam ever got anything else done in his life, with his butt hole needing that much attention all the time, all those big cocks and a never-ending supply of cum. He was a true fuck-pig, a hole to be bred.

Otis started getting up and buttoning his trousers. "Well, we better go check things out."

They led me up the stairs into a bright kitchen. It was morning outside, I figured…at least, the sun had fully risen. But I didn't know how long I was out. Shit, for all I knew it was the middle of the fuckin' afternoon.

Another goodlooking dude around Lamont's age, hispanic, was sitting at the kitchen table, playing cards. He looked up and smiled when we walked in. "Howdy fellas," he said. To me, he added: "You look mighty tired and worked over, there, little whoreboy. Set yourself down here, take a load off." Lamont spread out a dish towel over the seat of one of the chairs, and I sat on it while Otis brought me a cup of coffee. I took a sip, not even thinking they might be drugging me again. Turns out they weren't. Whatever they used me for, they were done now. I was naked and shivering in what looked like the kitchen of a shitty little ranch house, having coffee with total strangers who had spent the last several hours using my ass against my will.

"How's the other one?" Otis asked the guy at the table.

"Doing fine. He's mighty compliant after them young boys roughed him up some more and did their thing." The hispanic dude didn't even look at us while talking, just kept to his solitaire game. "You go on in there if you want. Think they're using him for stud service right now on little Rodney. After that, he'll be all done."

I had no idea what this meant, and I didn't want to leave my coffee, but after Lamont and Otis disappeared down the hall, I felt like I oughta follow. Besides, I wasn't gonna leave this house without Cameron, and I assumed that was who they were talking about. I oughta at least go check out how he was doing. Otis had hung a blanket over the back of my chair, so I stood up and wrapped that around myself to keep warm.

I walked down the hallway toward noises coming from a bedroom down at the end. The door was part way open, and I pushed it open slowly, not sure what I would find inside. Besides Otis and Lamont, there were two other guys in there just standing around, their flies open and hard black cocks sticking out. Then on the bed were three more: Kinzie, Cameron, and some lithe little light-skinned black boy who looked around 16.

Cameron's face was badly bruised. He had two black eyes, and the rest of his face looked pretty dark as well. His eyes were barely open. His lips were parted and covered with spit and dried blood. He lay on his back in the middle of the mattress, which was covered in a big square black rubber mat. The bed was a four-poster, and each of Cam's hands and legs were tied to the corners by lengths of rope. Kinzie was between Cam's legs, pushing his fat black cock in and out of Cam's leaking, used pussy. Cam's sexy, slim muscular legs looked fuckin' hot bent around this black stud and then tied from the ankles to the bedposts.

The young kid was sitting over Cam's crotch, facing Kinzie and the foot of the bed, and looked like he was blissing out as he rode Cam's fat eight inches up and down really fast. I was impressed that Cam had a raging hardon at this point. Can't be easy getting turned on when a bunch of guys are punching your lights out, drugging you silly, and raping you at both ends for hours and hours. Or can it? Maybe this was the kind of shit Cam truly lived for. He was always a depraved slut whenever I saw him having sex, even though the rest of the time on campus he acted like your typical goofy, totally normal, hot frat guy. So when I noticed his rock hard dick, I wasn't worried any more. I had a feeling he secretly liked this shit a lot.

The hot little teen bottom was going absolutely crazy on Cam's fat cock. "Nn-nnye-eehhh... nn-yee-eeahh..." he grunted over and over, like a wild animal. This boy had a great little body goin' on: tight chest, strong legs, but almost hairless on both. He basically looked like any goodlookin' young black dude you see at the park playing basketball with his friends or whatever. Only he seemed to live for taking big dicks up his ass.

"Yeah, fuck 'im slut... fuck dat hot lil' pussy-boy..." said one of the black dudes who was beating off. "Give our lil' nigger bitch some o' that good white bone... fill up his ass with some o' dat college love juice..."

Otis, standing next to me, leaned over and explained quietly: "Rodney here's our full-time bitch boy. He lives in this house and we fuck him whenever we want. Me, Lamont, his friends, our friends...everybody."

I gulped. What a life that would be. "How old is he?" I had to ask.

"Nineteen, now. Just turned," Otis said, first having to think for a minute. "Had his birthday a little while back. Came to us a year back I believe. Runaway. Lamont picked him up down by the docks. He's a good boy. Gotta fine, soft little hole. And he lo-o-oves dick. He gets loads and loads from us, every single day."

Fuckin' incredible. These creepy dudes not only drug and rape college boys like Cam and me, they're into taking in runaway kids, as well. Then again, I was having a lot of sex at his age, too. Younger, even. Just not like little Rodney. Maybe this was the life he wanted. Living here with a roof over his head, at least.

Then Lamont spoke. "You, now," he said to me. "Go over to your friend."

I didn't move, I just blinked. I was a little afraid what he might want me to do, but I was even more afraid of what might happen if I didn't do it.

"I said move it," Lamont growled, pointing with one hand and fumbling for his big dick with the other. He was getting hard again, I could tell. I walked over to the side of the bed, letting my blanket fall to the floor. Cam turned his head and looked at me, groggy and slobbering. "Now. Stick your dick in his mouth."

Fuck. Really? I couldn't do that. Cam never touched me before, after all, and I ain't never touched him.

"Do it," Lamont commanded. I looked in Lamont's eyes. They were burning. He fuckin' meant business.

I looked back at Cam, raising my eyebrows, like: This gonna happen? I searched his face for a reply, but the thing was he was so fuckin' beat up he could barely manage any expression anyway. Then I thought about all the shit that already happened, and that was still happening. What was one more little humiliation.

So I climbed onto the bed, positioning myself on my knees next to Cam's face. Without hesitating for a second, he twisted his head toward me and sucked my cock into his mouth. To my surprise, I was already half hard. My cock felt a little rough going over his bruised lips, but his mouth was soft and wet and warm. He was a devoted cocksucker, pushing himself with his neck up and down my shaft. Even at that awkward angle, and even being in the middle of a hot fuck sandwich like he was, Cameron gave me excellent head.

The other guys in the room seemed to appreciate the scene, too. Lamont pulled on his dick again, which had just shot up my ass a short while earlier, and started beating off alongside his two friends. Otis did not follow suit, which I was kind of happy about—but then again, if you told me an old guy's cock would taste that good, I never woulda believed you before this, anyway. Whatever, he just watched all of us and smiled.

I looked down at Cam's chest. His six-pack and tan muscles looked superfine as always, but they looked even hotter covered in sweat and cum and…something else? Plus, he had bruises from what looked like a couple of gut punches, which I gotta admit kinda turned me on. Before long I was long-dicking my rock hard cock in and out of his sucking face, and grunting shit at him: "Yeah, eat it Cam, eat that cock boy…"

Cam just kept on sucking. I focused on his handsome, submissive, beat-up face for a bit, then shifted my gaze over to Rodney's fine little teen ass, still bouncing up and down on Cam's cock a hundred miles a minute. Rodney was wailing like a bitch and hanging onto Kinzie's strong shoulders for support. I couldn't see Kinzie that well, but I saw the motions his huge muscular black ass was making back and forth as he pistoned his giant dick in and out of Cam's hole, and I knew my buddy was getting the fucking of his life.

Inspired now, I amped up the dirty talk with Cam, wanting to see where it got me. "Fuck dude, do it…eat my cock you dirty bitch…" Sure enough, Cam doubled his efforts. His sexual energy seemed like it knew no limits. No wonder he was such a natural whore. "Fuckin' suck it, dude…I want your fuckin' pussy mouth on my dick, just like that… fuck, oh fu-u-ucck yeah…yeah, do it stud, fuckin' eat me…wanna drop this load, spray it right in your mouth…gonna make you eat this load, fucker…you fuckin' sorry ass horny lil' bitch…"

Cam's blowjob was incredible, and the scene made it even hotter. I was getting close, but I wasn't there yet. With a roar, Kinzie was the first to cum, screaming as his hot black sperm erupted into Cam's beautiful ass.

"Oh-h! FU-U-UCCK!" Kinzie bellowed. "Uh-hnnh, ah fuck…take all this nigger cum, white fuckin' slut—"

This kicked off a chain reaction in the room. Little Rodney started screaming next that Cam was getting off inside him. "Oh-h! I feel it…

feel this white boy's cu-um-mm...I feel it goin' in my hole, way up inside me..."

Rodney didn't slow down, obviously wanting to milk Cam's bone for all he could get. I watched his hot little black ass continue moving up and down rapidly on Cam's thick white meat, and sure enough, juicy globs of cum started oozing and squirting out of Rodney's tight opening, as Cam's blunt tool plunged the load he was shooting in and out of the black kid's cute ass. Rodney lasted about thirty more seconds, then started beating off his own teen meat and shooting big ropes of jism straight up into the air. Some of it got on Kinzie, who had pulled out but was standing nearby. The rest of Rodney's cum fell on Cam's hot legs. The whole time he was cumming, Rodney kept Cam's rock hard cock buried the whole way up his ass.

Lamont, standing right where he was, pulled a few extra times on his big black knob and shot a load so straight and so forceful that it hit both Rodney and Cam in the chests, a good five feet or so away. Seeing the force behind Lamont's nut and knowing he'd shot it even more forcefully into my ass earlier made me suddenly lose control myself. I swooned a little, grabbing the wall to support myself, and then unloaded my seed right down into Cameron's sweet, sucking face, mouth and throat. He gulped down every last hot drop.

The last two dudes waddled over to the bed with their pants open and each dropped their load on Cameron's midsection. Their cocks were pretty average but they both shot nice, big goopy loads onto his six-pack abs.

Lamont walked over as well, even though he just came, and his dick was fairly soft. I wondered what he might be up to. Then I finally realized what else was on Cam's body and why the rubber mat was over the mattress. Lamont hung his dick over Cam's belly and started to piss, a long stream of piss that he lazily pointed up Cam's body at his face (still sucking my cock clean) and then back down across his chest and crotch.

Just as Lamont finished up, his two friends who had just cum followed suit, pissing all over Cam.

I was wide-eyed with shock. I'd never seen anyone get pissed on before, much less a hot frat type like my buddy Cameron. But the next sensation surprised me even more: I wanted to do it, too. Now that I had cum, I realized how badly I needed to piss—god only knows the last time I'd even been inside a bathroom. But I wanted to piss on Cam, just like the other guys had done. I had no idea if it was cool with them, or Cam…?

Looking down at Cam's face, I got my answer. He had released my still-hard cock from his mouth and was kissing the last drops of cum off the tip. He saw my expression and managed a weak smile, and a nod. Then he did something else: he opened his mouth a little wider, tipped his head back slightly, and shut his eyes. Holy shit! He wanted me to piss in his mouth. I couldn't control myself, and I accidentally started to piss, letting loose with a couple of spurts that arced up over Cam's head and landed on his face. He licked his lips and hungrily swallowed, then looked sideways at me, nodding again, begging almost, wanting more.

Fuck, OK, here goes. I got up on my haunches again and pointed my piss hard-on at his face, then let it fly. To my relief, the guys in the room cheered me on. I had so much in my bladder, I think I peed on Cam for over two minutes. A lot of it got in his mouth, but he couldn't keep up with swallowing it, so it ended up dribbling down his chin and pooling at his neck. When I finally finished, I stuck my cock back in Cam's mouth so he could get the last drops of piss off it. Even though my boner gradually did go down over the course of emptying my bladder, Cam cleaned me up so well I swear at the end I started getting hard again.

When I looked up again, a couple of the guys were starting to untie Cam's bonds. Rodney left the room and came back with our clothes, throwing them onto Cam's chest in a heap, including our sneakers, a couple of which tumbled onto the carpeted floor. Throwing the whole pile onto Cam's filthy body obviously got piss and cum all over our clothes, but no one seemed to care much, so we didn't either. My white jockstrap was in the pile, as was Cam's red jockstrap. I guess they'd pulled them off us at some point when we were getting used. Our jeans and T-shirts were wadded up into sticky balls of cloth. I have no idea where the bag went that I took to the frat house, with the lube pump and the extra towels. Without a word spoken, we both got dressed and made our way out the front door of the house. We didn't say anything to Otis or Lamont.

Out in the street, we walked to the nearest intersection. We were in a residential neighborhood somewhere on the far side of town. I didn't even recognize the names on the street sign. We paused there a moment. Cam fished in his jeans pocket for his phone, and we both waited while it powered up.

"Quarter to 5pm," he said. He looked at a couple of text messages, then stuffed the phone back in his jeans.

"Now what," I said. I could smell the piss, cum and sweat that had covered Cam. It was now on my collar.

"My truck's parked over there," he said, a bit of info that seemed totally fuckin' incongruous, I gotta say. He started off walking down the sidewalk, and sure enough, there was his ratty pickup parked at the curb, a half-block in the distance.

"What the fuck," I said. "Did Lamont and them drive it over? Or what the fuck?"

"Nah, I parked it here yesterday, before the party started. Before I came and got you."

No shit. "Uh, buddy…" I didn't know what to say. "So…uh, you knew all this was gonna happen?"

We got in the truck. Cam looked in the rear view mirror at his cut lips, his swollen eyes. Then he sighed.

"I knew something was gonna go down like this, yeah. I worked it out with the frat dudes. Figured it would be on this level. I've tussled with Lamont and a few of his rough-type boys before. They're regulars."

Holy fuck. I couldn't believe this. I don't know what was more un-fuckin'-believable—the fact that Cam had willingly let himself get abducted and gang raped, or the fact that he'd let me get involved, as well.

Sensing my pissiness, he turned and looked right at me. "Look, I told them to take it easy with you. Play it by ear. You're new to all this. I told them all to just watch your reactions, go at your pace. But then I knew, once they had you on board, they'd probably take it as far as they could. They're like that."

"On board? They fuckin' drugged me, man."

Cam smiled. "Yeah, I thought they might do that." He started the truck and we began winding our way out of that neighborhood, back to a main road. "Look, it's one of those things. You're in it a little, you might as well go the distance. They didn't beat you up at all, did they? I mean, besides a few smacks on your ass?"

I made a sour expression, facing hotly out the windshield. "I dunno man. I haven't checked for bruises."

"Well, they didn't. Lamont said they wouldn't, so they didn't. That was the limit I set up."

"Oh thanks."

We continued in silence. About fifteen minutes later he was dropping me back at the dorm. I had no idea what I looked like, having been fucked repeatedly for nearly 24 hours, but I didn't care either. I just wanted to get a shower and get into my bed. Before I got out of the truck, though, I had to ask one last question.

"So what did we make off this little adventure, oh mentor of mine?"

Cam, his puffed-up face looking like a boxer's coming out of a fuckin' TKO, managed to flash one of his big, dumb, toothy smiles. "Oh, a whole fuckin' lot, I'd say. Everything that happened, we split fifty-fifty. And Lamont's crew is paying double for all the crazy shit they wanted, believe me. That was the deal."

"OK, so how much are we talking."

"Otis said there was gonna be 50 guys total coming and going at his place, and they all paid him $400 each. You and me, we split half of that, and Otis keeps the other half for himself. That's ten grand for us, total. Five goes in your pocket, five goes in mine. And that's not counting all the coin we got at the frat party."

Holy god on earth. The life of a college boy slut. For all that, I made between five and seven thousand bucks. Not too shabby. I didn't wanna do it again any time soon, and I still couldn't quite wrap my head around the idea that I'd been pimped out without my knowledge by some old black grandpa named Otis. But the money…the money was why I was in this in the first place. Right? And this was good money.

I got out of the truck, looking back at my friend as I held the door open. His bruises were nasty, but from what he was telling me, he'd been roughed up like that before. "You gonna be alright, man?" I asked him.

"Yeah," he said, checking himself in the mirror again. "Kinzie's boys are pretty good at playing rough without doing much lasting damage. Don't worry, man, this'll all clear up in a couple of days."

A couple of days. "What are ya gonna tell everyone about what happened to your face?" I wondered.

He laughed. "Same thing I always say. That I was in a bar, I was loaded, and couldn't shut my fuckin' mouth." He revved the truck engine. "You know, in a way, some of that shit is even true."

I smiled and rolled my eyes. Sick fuck. Then I slammed the truck door shut and watch Cam pull away.

(9)

DUDE

I went up to my dorm room, did some sit-ups, and ate a power bar. I was fuckin' ravenous, but I could barely stay awake. In fact, I don't even remember going to sleep. I don't think I've been that exhausted in my whole entire life. I remember thinking I should take a shower (I totally reeked of cum and sweat) but then the next thing I knew I woke up several hours later, around midnight probably, on my bed with all my clothes still on. I kinda panicked at first in the pitch dark, thinking half-awake that I was still in the john's basement across town. But when I figured out I was home I just pulled off my disgusting jeans and T-shirt, slid under the covers, and blacked out.

Next morning, I woke up like a shot. I must have slept really soundly because my whole body actually felt refreshed. I still smelled of sex but hey, that wasn't the worst smell to wake up to. The sun was coming in through the ratty blinds on my dorm room window. I couldn't see my watch anywhere but I guess it was around 7 o'clock. I wasn't usually up at this hour but something woke me, and it took me a second to figure out what it was…

My ass. It felt like it was on fire. Sore, yeah, from all the business it got the previous day. But mostly, it was just twitching like crazy. As if getting fucked constantly for almost 24 hours had somehow reset it in "receive" mode. I felt healthy and awake, but totally empty down below. I absolutely needed to be fucked, and soon. It was literally impossible to concentrate on anything else until that happened.

I put my hand down there and started finger banging myself. The stimulation felt nice. There was still a ton of dried jizz around the edge, and plenty of liquid cum oozed out around my fingers once I started pushing them in and out. It felt nice, but it wasn't enough. Frantic, I looked around the dorm room for something I could use as a dildo. The only thing in sight was the bar for the dumbbell set that I used for doing curls. From the bed, I reached over and rolled the dumbbell toward me, and quickly stripped the weights off on either end, leaving just the bar. Second later the bar was fully up my ass. My eyes shut and I let out a sigh of relief. Penetration felt like a balm on my open wound. Lazily I slid the bar in and out of me in deep, long strokes, getting just about a whole foot of the thing inside me. I kept it going and tried to pretend I was getting fucked. But the bar was only an inch thick or so. It was no substitute for real cock.

So after a few minutes of this, I said: Fuck it. I grabbed my phone from the pocket of my jeans, which were still in a pile on the dorm room floor. But even with the phone in my hand, I just stared at it like an idiot. Who the fuck was I gonna call? Usually the johns called me. In fact, that was always what happened. I didn't have any regulars lined up for that whole day, because I figured I'd need time to bounce back from the party (even before I found out what a fuckin' crazy event that was gonna be). Thinking some guys might have tried to reach me anyways, I checked my text messages: Zero. Voicemail: Nothing. Fuck.

I went back to beating off. I'd woken up with a gargantuan hard-on that felt like it was twice as big and twice as hard as the one I usually woke up with most mornings. I pulled my pud like a fuckin' madman with one hand while I kept on ramming the weights bar up my hole with the other. I shut my eyes again and visualized the party. Getting my ass rammed non-stop by all those hot fuckin' fratboys. Getting my hole felched by Jeremy, the dream stud. Watching Cam go absolutely ape-shit crazy for dicks, in both his holes, over and over and over, like no cock-crazed bitch I had ever met or even heard of. Getting drugged and raped and used repeatedly by an ever-expanding gang of black and latino studs. Thinking of Cam getting…

That was it, I had to call Cam. No way was I gonna cum without some kinda cock up my ass. I wasn't saying Cam had to fuck me. I just figured he'd know what to do. Shit, after the stunt he'd pulled on me by arranging the after-party with Kinzie and them, he fuckin' owed me big time. I found his name and called.

"Yeah?" He sounded zonked out when he picked up. I figured I probably woke him.

"Sorry to get you up man."

"You didn't, dude. I'm getting fucked really hard right now. Can I call you back in a little bit?"

Unreal. "Uh…" I pictured Cam getting pounded by dick, which was what I wanted more than anything.

"C'mon buddy, what's up?"

"I gotta get some cock," I blurted out. "I'm goin' fuckin' crazy over here, I dunno what's going on. I woke up and my ass just needs it. You gotta help me out. Send someone over here to fuck me. Right away."

There was a pause. I heard Cam's top grunting in the background, but Cam just breathed heavily while he figured out his response. "Yeah, OK," he said finally. "Give me, like, twenty minutes. I'll be right over."

———————

Nineteen minutes later, there was a knock on my door. I pulled the weights bar out of my hole—it was covered with lube and cum—and set it on top of my dresser, then walked over to answer the door. I was still wearing my jizz-covered jockstrap from the previous day's adventures.

Cam walked in, followed by a familiar and welcome sight: some tall blond dude, a real hunk. I recognized him from the quad—he was an upperclassman and a jock, totally goodlooking.

"This is Kai," Cam said. "He's gonna fuck you."

Fuckin' awesome. As Kai got undressed, I asked Cam: "That's short notice, dude. What was he doing up?"

"He's always up early. He's the one I call when I do what you do, wake up horny and need a big cock."

Kai stepped forward. He was fuckin' beautiful. Deep tan, perfect chest, light and even covering of hair on his pecs and legs, sexy little treasure trail connecting his slim tummy and his rock-hard ten-inch dick.

He flashed me a big, cute smile. "Arright, little man, let's get you fucked."

"How do you want me?"

"Get on your back."

I laid back down on my messy bed, and once I'd found a comfortable position, I spread my jock legs wide. Kai slipped between them, and I was in agony for the few seconds it took him to prep himself. He spit in his hand a few times, and rubbed his dick to get it to max hardness. Neither of these were necessary as far as I was concerned but I tried to wait patiently. Then I felt the bliss of his big dickhead pushing through my starving hole, and without any further bullshit, he slid his whole shaft straight up into my ass.

The sound I made just then is hard to describe. I guess it must have been like some kind of animal. It was close to some of the depraved noises I'd heard Cam make at the party. All I can say is, taking Kai's cock right then was just the best fuckin' thing I could have imagined. My strangled cry turned into a sort of whimper. I felt like such a slutty little bitch. Both guys were kinda snickering at me but I didn't care.

"You like that, I guess," Kai said.

"Oh yeah..." I panted. "Fuckin' A, dude...gimme that...oh fuck..."

Kai started moving in and out, and already I needed to explode. I reached into my jock and hammered on my cock while looking up through blurry eyes at his blue eyes and rockin' body. I gave a little scream and started squirting my pent-up load of cum all over myself. Kai just kept on fucking.

"Oh fuck... oh fuck..." I babbled.

Cam smiled at me. "Think he needed that one, man."

"Yeah," Kai said, picking up the pace on my ass, dredging his big tool deeper inside with every thrust. He was a fuckin' excellent fuck. "You want this, huh? You want this, you sick horny depraved little fucker?"

"Fuck yeah. Fuck me dude. I want all your cum in my hole. Fuck me as hard as you can."

Without asking, Cam got on the bed next to me, opened his jeans, and stuck his cock in my face. It wasn't hard yet, but I totally wanted to suck it anyway. All of the weirdness about us being friends was gone. I guess the sexual extravaganza we'd taken part in had caused us to shed those last few inhibitions. I took him in my mouth and sucked his knob like a piece of candy. It was fuckin' great to feel it expand in my mouth. Before long he had a raging boner and was dripping precum all over my tongue, so he grabbed my head and started face-fucking me so hard I thought he was gonna dislocate my fuckin' throat. So sweet.

I got fucked at both ends like that until I sensed Kai was ready to cum. I spat out Cam's dick and looked up at Kai again. His big hands were gripping my calves and holding them out in front while his pile-driver of a dick pushed harder and harder into my male twat. He looked like a fuckin' god, riding my ass hard like that.

"Yeah dude… use my hole, c'mon… oh just fuck it… ah, fuck, that feels good man… fuck it deep and fill me up with seed…"

"Yeah? You want this load?" he asked. It's fuckin' hot when guys ask me that. The answer is always yes.

"Fuck yes man. Fuck your load in me. I wanna feel it. Now."

Sure enough, he sprung like a geyser into me. I could feel his load spraying me from the inside as Kai dumped all his gooey cum syrup in my hole. There's nothing quite like a wake-up fuck from a hung jock who fucks like a pro and shoots a huge load in your ass. I hoped Kai would become a regular for me, too.

"Feel that load?" he whooped.

"Oh fuck yeah I do," I moaned. It was so fuckin' gratifying to get fresh cum in my ass when I'd been crazy for it such a short time before. Cam really came through on this one. Shit, I could still feel Kai shooting. His orgasm went on forever. "Oh fuck, that's a good load… thank you man… thank you so much…"

Kai and Cam switched places so I could clean up my new jock friend. As I was eating all that good cum sauce off Kai's dick, Cam slipped his knob in my hole and started taking his sloppy seconds. It shoulda been a big moment, I guess, taking my buddy and mentor's big dick up my ass, but it actually felt pretty casual at that point. I was so happy to get fucked by Kai it was almost unreal, so I had no problem giving Cam a little "thank-you" fuck if he wanted to unload in me there as well.

And soon enough, that's what he did. Cam's cum escaped into me just as I was licking the last remnants of Kai's load off his horse cock, which was still half-hard. I was vaguely aware that I was probably gonna miss my morning class, and it felt a little embarrassing to be giving up my hole for free like this (especially to Cam) but at that moment I didn't really care. I was just glad I'd gotten what I needed so bad.

Kai grabbed his gym bag and took off, and Cam laid down beside me. We dozed a little more, both of us needing to restore some energy from the sex party madness. Now, I have just a twin bed, so it was a little weird at first to have Cam so close to me, but I'd done the same thing with Freddie a few times when he was too stoned to go back to his room after I blew him or we fucked, so I didn't think too much of it.

But when I woke up again around 10:30, Cam had actually snuggled against me, his arm on my chest and his face pressed against the side of my chest. Instinctively, I elbowed him. "Dude, wake up. Move over."

Cam grunted a little, then burrowed his face into me further. I figured he was a deep sleeper, but then I looked down at his face and I saw he was smiling. What the fuck? "Move over," I repeated, and gave him a shove. He opened his eyes and looked up at me, still smiling. It was cute, but I didn't want to say so. He finally rolled onto his back next to me, filling the space between me and the window.

We were silent for a couple of minutes. The sun was mostly blocked out by the blinds now, so I figured Cam had closed them while we were napping. He'd also pulled a blanket up over both our bodies.

"Dude," he said simply. "Dude…"

I somehow knew what was coming next, or I roughly did. My body tensed up. I didn't say anything. I shut my eyes, as if I was going back to sleep.

"Dude, we gotta talk, man." Cam reached over and put his hand on my thigh. His touch was firm, but still gentle. I felt a rush when he touched me like that, and immediately I started to relax. I also felt a little lightheaded. But I still didn't say much.

"What."

My eyes were still shut but I knew he was looking right at me. Slowly I opened them and turned my head to the side. Cam was gazing at me with the sweetest, most tender look I've ever seen from any guy. His eyes were still puffy but the bruising had gone down a bit. He was right, the lumps healed fast on him. He had such a beautiful face. Hard to believe I'd never noticed before. But then, I'd never seen it this close up.

He didn't say anything, just smiled. He was relaxed. He shifted a little so he could prop his head up with one hand and face me more directly. The look on his face said he wasn't going any place anytime soon.

I figured his game was to make me say whatever was next, but I had no idea what that was. Fuck, I didn't even know how I was feeling right then. Most of my sensations lately were all around sex. And speaking of that, the next thing I was aware of was—you guessed it—my ass. It was tingling, like it always did, but now in kinda a different way. That part of my body had become such a huge part of my life now. My money maker, my secret weapon. My hard, jock ass. Packed with cum. Cam's cum. I felt fuckin' vibrant suddenly.

And then I knew exactly what came next. With the most natural of forces, like gravity, I leaned my body toward Cam's. My face arrived right at his, and I kissed him. It felt like something totally new. I still hadn't kissed a guy, any guy, except for that quick peck that Clayton put on me just before all the afterparty shit went down. And now I was kissing Cam. Mind you, I'd fucked his face, even pissed on him, and I just took his big load right up my ass that morning. But kissing him was different, more special. It felt unreal. It was just a few seconds at first, and I started to pull back, but then he leaned into me the same way, and we were off. We couldn't stop. He was masterful. Soon his hands were all over me, and I responded by wrapping myself around his strong body and holding him on top of me as we kept on making out. Fuck, I didn't want it to ever end. I've never in my whole life been kissed like that, and I never even wanted it half as much.

At some point I felt one of Cam's hands disappear for a minute. We kept on kissing, but I wondered what was up. I felt around the back of him and realized he was putting a couple of fingers up his ass. Not just that, but he grabbed my hand and put it down there, too, just to make sure I knew what he was doing and what he obviously wanted. Fuckin' hot. Again, totally new. I'm the fuckin' power bottom here…ain't no guy I've been with ever given me a signal like that. But I was ready. I rolled us so Cam was underneath me and I climbed on top of him, between his spread sexy legs. I lined up my rock hard cock with his fleshy hole, and in one thrust I sunk it fully inside. Not surprisingly, it felt as good as any place my dick had ever been, ever. Wet, welcoming, luscious, and ready. Lubed with juice. Cam's boy cooze felt like the ultimate hole.

As I pounded him deep and steady, we kept on kissing. Not just kissing, but using our muscles to pull ourselves together, like we were destined to just be one body. My hands went everywhere…his neck, his face, the top of his head, all the way down his sexy chest and muscular jock back to the perky globes of his fine college ass. I remembered hearing him whimper at the party when he got fucked hard, so I started fucking him harder and harder until he made those sounds again. I was vaguely aware that his hole had been used and abused repeatedly for most of the preceding couple of days, just like mine had. But any concern about that melted away when I realized—I knew—that he loved it and wanted it as much as I did.

Over and over I fucked him. I came in his ass, flipped him over, and fucked him again. We fell off the bed, onto the floor, and fucked like that for a while. Then standing up, against the closet. Then back on the bed again. I fucked Cam's ass so hard he was almost screaming at one point. There was some pounding on the walls and (I think) the door, but we just ignored it. He wailed like a bitch as I throttled his fine ass in every different position we could come up with. I fucked him so hard that he shot two loads of cum on himself without touching his cock, both right in a row.

Then I dumped another load in him, and that slowed us down a little, but not for long. Cam sucked me until I was hard again, and then he sat right down on my shaft, using his fuckin' excellent legs to hoist himself up and down on my dick, fucking himself with my cock like the depraved slut I knew he was. Like this, he could kiss me again, so I just relaxed and made out with him while he did the work. Our embrace was so mesmerizing that after a little while, I felt my cum escaping up into his beautiful, talented hole once more.

Following that, it seemed only natural to let Cam take his turn again. He got me on my back and pounded me with his sweet hard cock. I flopped around like a rag doll and beat off two more loads while he was inside me. The whole time, we kept our lips together and continued making out. I did more kissing that day than I've done in my whole life, and that's sayin' something. I laid back and just let my hot friend take over.

Finally, around mid-afternoon, we were exhausted. We fell in a heap on my bed once again, pretty much where we'd started, only now several hours had passed, and we were even more covered with sweat and cum than we'd been before. Also, one other important difference was obvious: The two of us felt something bonding us, something more than buddy-buddy, mentor-student. We weren't just a couple of college studs any more. We were two buttboys in love.

We cuddled and napped again. I think I actually smiled while I slept. I felt such total and complete peace.

When I woke again, the sun was almost down. I nudged Cam, and he kissed me, half-awake.

"Dude," I said. I didn't know what else to say. It was just too awesome. Just: "Dude."

He seemed to understand completely. We made out a little, and then he sat up.

"You horny?"

I laughed at him. "You fuckin' kidding? We just fucked the whole day, man. Your ass has got to be just overflowing right about now."

Cam gave me a cute smirk. "Yeah, dude. But, guys like us? We just fuckin' can't get enough. Right?"

He was right. My ass was aching for cock. My own cock was so hard it was sore. I just smiled as my reply.

"Get up," he said. "There's a whole world waiting out there. We can go out and I can show you the sights."

"The sights?"

"Tea rooms. Glory holes. This town's full of action. I'll even take you to the truck stop later. It's about ten miles out, along the highway. Tons of big cocks and hot trucker cum, ready to shoot." My mind reeled. "Trust me, man, you can get all the dick you want up there. I'll get you fucked like you won't believe."

I watched Cam get dressed. I was in awe of this dude. He was right. It was suddenly pretty obvious that we loved each other—and believe me, it felt pretty weird to even think that about another guy—but we also both totally loved dick. We fuckin' craved it, even. We were addicted. From that day on, even while I went about being the same dude I always was, I would also be a one-hundred-percent buttboy, willing and needing to give up my sweet ass to guys' cocks. Cam's felt special, but any cock would do. There would be pussy, yes, and frat parties and bar hopping, all the usual macho stuff, but he and I had a special bond, not just because of our mutual feelings but because we had discovered the truth: We totally needed cocks and cum to live.

(10)

CAM

From that point on, things have been fuckin' awesome. I didn't know where life was leading me, but I knew one thing: I would follow Cam anywhere. The last few months had been the greatest adventure of my life.

And in the months that have passed since then, life has only gotten better. Cam's in love with me, and I'm totally nuts about him as well. We're together just about all the time. It's more than a sexual thing, I guess, but sex is a big part of it. I sleep at Cam's room, or he sleeps at mine. I fuck him every night before we go to sleep (he says he can't sleep now without my load in his ass) and in the morning, whoever wakes up first just starts fucking the other. Beats the hell outa an alarm clock. Then we get up, go to classes or whatever, and by the end of the day we're usually trekking out to get more dick. He has his regulars, and so do I. I get 4 or 5 loads most nights from paying customers, which is good pocket money. Cam has always charged more so he makes out even better. Then we usually meet up again at his dorm, where he keeps a stash of toys. We like to put butt plugs in our asses to keep the cum inside longer. After that, we head out for more.

The truck stop he talked about is currently my favorite place. Whatever ideas I had about truckers being old and fat and smelly, I've totally gotten over it now. I mean, some of them are that way, but it can still be really hot. But actually, a lot of them are fit dudes who just happen to be ten or twenty years older than us, and trust me, they fuckin' know what to do with their cocks. Most of them are just fuckin' happy to have any kind of action swinging on their dicks after a few days of travel. The fact that we're college buttboy cum dumps just makes it even better, as far as they're concerned. And there are plenty of others like us who show up, too: college boys, even some high schoolers, and then just random horny gay guys a little older than us from around the area. I'd say half the time I take trucker loads, and the rest I get from other guys.

Needless to say, Cam goes totally wild at the truck stop, especially when there's plenty of action already taking place. He just gets out there in the middle of it. There are a few back rooms in the main building where the staff just leaves you alone, and beyond that there's the woods. The cops show up sometimes but the staff can see them coming and there's plenty of time to get your clothes back on and cover your tracks.

At the truck stop, Cam always gives his ass away for free. I don't usually charge the truckers, but once in a while they slip me some cash anyway. I'm just that good, I guess (ha). The other dudes who fuck me there sometimes recognize me as the buttboy from campus and they offer to pay the usual charge, which is cool.

There's a lot of voyeur action, too, and Cam and I love to show off. Not many guys realize that Cam and I are together (like a couple, or whatever) so they think it's even hotter when we "hook up" in front of them. Typically after I take a bunch of loads in my ass or down my throat, I need to get off myself, and since my favorite place to do that is Cam's asshole, I'll seek him out and pump it into him, giving him all my sperm. Since he's nothing but a fuckin' depraved cum pig at that place, he just takes it and begs for more. The other guys always love watching this part. Just last week, I saw Cam on his back in one of the rooms, giving head to a guy who was fucking his face. I got between Cam's legs, put his knees up over my shoulders, and started fucking him. This drew a crowd, and while I continued banging my hot buddy's sweet hole, five or six guys all beat off onto Cam's sexy chest. He was covered in cum and loving it. Then I sprayed my cum into his ass, and got back on my knees in the other room to get fucked by a bunch of skate-rat type punks.

Another hot thing I'm just catching onto is all the verbal stuff. Cam's really good at it. He can beg for dick and say lots of other wild stuff but he still manages to sound fairly manly while he's doing it. (Well, most of the time. Sometimes he whimpers like a fuckin' girl, which weirdly is kinda hot, too.) He was in the woods behind the truck stop one time getting his bent-over ass pounded by this muscular older dude with a nice trim beard. I heard Cam say something like, "That's my cum hole, daddy…please put your load in there…" and it got me instantly hard. His pitch was low, pretty much his normal voice, and yet he was being totally submissive. He went on like that: "Ooh yeah, gimme that hot load, daddy…breed your boy…" and then, when the guy finally shot off, Cam said: "Thank you for your cum, daddy…it feels so good inside my ass…"

That stuck with me, and a few days later, I was tricking for this skinny kid who usually stopped by my dorm room but on this day was meeting me at his "older friend's" house a few miles away. This was a cool scene for me, as long as they both paid, which they did, and it turned out to be especially nice because his friend was a superhot daddy type: fortyish, good worked-out body, trim goatee—basically the "hot coach" type that lots of the gay boys seem to want, and I was starting to understand why. Plus, the dude was packing a true ten inches, which on his older frame looked even better than usual. As soon as I saw his meat, I knew I was gonna totally bitch out for him, too. Me and the other kid got on our knees, and while we took turns sucking the guy's dick, I started in with a little of the daddy talk, just to see how it worked.

"Yeah…you gotta real nice dick, daddy…" I said softly. It was true. It looked sweet going in and out of the kid's mouth, right in front of my eyes. The precum was oozing out around the kid's lips. I licked my chops.

I didn't know if what I said was cool or not, but it musta been, because the hunky older dude responded right away. "Then eat it, boy," he said, sort of a low growl, pulling out of my other trick's mouth, entering mine, and laying his fat slab right onto my tongue. "Suck daddy's dick. You like that." He was right, I did. I was also starting to realize the turn-on of being with a dude who knows what he wants and just takes it.

I hummed and gurgled. His cock was delicious. While I sucked, the other kid picked up some of the banter.

"Yeah, suck Daddy's cock…" he said, his voice a little bit girlier than mine. "I wanna feel it in my hole."

I was a little confused by this, as I thought I was the one getting fucked by the daddy, but I didn't care too much. The kid actually had a fine little skater body and it would be hot to watch his friend fuck him. So I just kept on sucking. Turns out we were both wrong, because after a bit more sloppy head, the older dude got us both on his bed together, with the kid behind me, and then sat in a chair in the corner to watch us.

"I wanna see you fuck this little stud," he said to his younger friend. Fine with me; the kid also had a real nice cock. I reached back between my legs and helped him guide it into me. He fumbled a little bit—I don't think he was a top very often—but I knew exactly how to help guys like him, and before long he was off and running, grabbing my hips and wildly pounding his teen-age boner frantically in and out of my hole.

"You like that, boy?" said the guy in the corner. I looked over. He was slowly pulling on his massive rod.

The kid fucking me practically squealed. "Oh yes daddy! His ass feels so-o-oo good…"

"Not you. You," he said, and I knew he meant me, because the whole time he never took his eyes off me.

"Yes, daddy," I said, trying to sound obedient but still like the frat dude I was. "Make him fuck me hard!"

"You heard him," he responded, talking to the kid. "Pound his ass, boy." He picked up the pace jerking off and looked back at me with a sly grin. "Yeah, he's fuckin' you real good. Does it feel good, do you like it?"

"Yes daddy! His cock feels so good!" And it did, too. I wasn't lying. This kid had some game.

"You like his big teen cock inside you? Slammin' your hot little hole?"

"Oh yes daddy…" and after that I just kept babbling, because it actually felt so good I was starting to feel a little weak. I think it was actually saying those words, making myself submissive to this older dude, that made me suddenly just want to relax and totally submit to him. To both of them, really. Daddy and his boy.

What else? Oh yeah, Cam took me to a sex club once. I can't wait to go back. It's in a bigger city, about two hours from our college town, so getting there and back means taking time off from school work and our paying clients. Still, it was quite a fuckin' treat. I left Cam at the glory holes, just inside the door, and went and found the sling room. It was awesome, bigger and more comfortable than the ones I'd sat in at the frat party, or the one I used in Kelan's friend's basement that time. I climbed in and fingered my hole, waiting for some tops. Traffic was a little slow at first, but soon as word got out there was a goodlooking, college-age bareback muscle boy cum dump hole lookin' for as many loads up his ass as he could get, the scene was pretty much set for a fuckin' all-night cum-and-go extravaganza. I didn't leave the sling at all until Cam showed up (leaking from both ends of course) and we got outa there, probably like six hours later.

Other than that, there are the glory holes all around campus, and the occasional gangbang party. We haven't done one quite as intense as the huge frat party where we were the center of attention, but I keep hearing that another event like that might be in the works. Whether we let it go as far as last time is still a subject of some debate. Cam's all for it, and we definitely picked up some serious coin, but I'm kinda uneasy about giving up that much control. I haven't been back to meet with Otis or Lamont, and they haven't gotten in touch with us either. I do see Rodney, their bitch boy, hanging around the campus tea rooms, sucking dick.

Speaking of the infamous frat party...we definitely expanded our fan base that evening, not to mention picking up a whole lot of new clientele. I had to get an iPhone to keep track of all my appointments. Pretty often, now, I have to squeeze in johns between classes, so when I leave in the morning, having a mobile thingie like that helps me plan out my route for that day: go to class here, stop by this dorm and get fucked, then to this class over here, and so on. It can get complicated and slightly stressful, but who am I kidding— planning it out just means more cocks and more loads for me. I can't go more than a few hours without dick anyway. My ass gets to twitching and it drives me nuts. In fact, if I have a spare half-hour between classes and no johns are scheduled, pretty often I'll hit the nearest campus glory hole anyway, usually some far-off men's room in one of the classroom buildings, to suck some good college cock and (hopefully) take a nice steamy load or two up in my hot jock ass. I've gotten it down to a few minutes in some cases: in, then out.

It's a pretty sweet life. I'm keeping up just fine with my classes, but my extracurricular time is spent with my new hobby, which is also my current livelihood of sorts. I'm known around campus as the "forty dollar buttboy" which has a nice ring to it, so I guess it's unlikely I'll ever raise my rate. That's fine—this started out being about the money, but now it's about something else. I've long since paid off the girl who had my kid, and I've got a bank account that's growing faster than I can keep track. So as long as I've got my spare cash for goin' out and getting blasted with my buddies on week-ends, I'm perfectly fine with my current profit margin. All that matters, really, is making Cam happy, and keeping my ass filled with dick and cum.

As for the future—well, who knows about that shit, anyway. My sophomore year is almost up. If I keep going like this I'll have no problem graduating in a few more years, probably with honors even. Cam isn't quite the student I am, but he's twice the businessman, so he's already cooking up more and more future schemes: expanding our operations; maybe buying a house to use so that we can host our own parties, and the rest of the time, tricks can come and go around the clock. I listen to his ideas, and some of them seem cool, but really he knows as long as I'm getting what I want (him, and loads) it's all OK on my end.

The other day we were having lunch at the same cafeteria on campus where he'd started out giving me all those pointers. He was eating a sandwich, and I was starting at his lips. All I wanted to do right then was kiss him, and fuck his mouth. He caught me looking, smiled, and reached over to mess up my hair a little.

"Penny for your thoughts, stud," he said. He looked so cute just then. I wanted to kiss him all over. In fact, when he got playful like that, I just wanted to spend my whole life with him. He was so beautiful: that rockin' body, those deep brown eyes. I almost jumped him right there in the cafeteria. But, I kept it cool.

"Sorry," I told him, going back to my lunch, acting all coy. "Forty dollars, buddy. That's the going rate."

ABOUT THE AUTHOR

JACKMAN HILL

Jackman Hill is just another horny white guy with a boring day job who loves writing smut. *Forty-Dollar ButtBoy* is his first published book. He also writes gay erotic stories on the internet under the alias Backlash29.